D0172696

A GHOSTLY VISITOR . . .

"She just stared at me with those coal black eyes," Jan said. "They were so cold, so—mean. I think she was trying to frighten me. Everything was suddenly ice-cold. The room. The air. She kept staring at me. Lumps of coal on that dead white face. I screamed, and she vanished back into the wall. Just disappeared. Then I guess I screamed again."

"These old inns contain many mysteries," Simon said.

Books by R. L. Stine

Available from ARCHWAY Paperbacks

For orders other than by individual consumers, Archway Books grants a discount on the purchase of **10 or more** copies of single titles for special markets or premium use. For further details, please write to the Vice-President of Special Markets, Pocket Books, 1230 Avenue of the Americas, New York, NY 10020.

For information on how individual consumers can place orders, please write to Mail Order Department, Paramount Publishing, 200 Old Tappan Road, Old Tappan, NJ 07675.

FEAR STREET

SUPER CHILLER

Party Summer

R. L. STINE

AN ARCHWAY PAPERBACK
Published by POCKET BOOKS
New York   London   Toronto   Sydney   Tokyo   Singapore

The sale of this book without its cover is unauthorized. If you purchased this book without a cover, you should be aware that it was reported to the publisher as "unsold and destroyed." Neither the author nor the publisher has received payment for the sale of this "stripped book."

This book is a work of fiction. Names, characters, places and incidents are either the product of the author's imagination or are used fictitiously. Any resemblance to actual events or locales or persons, living or dead, is entirely coincidental.

AN ARCHWAY PAPERBACK *Original*

An Archway Paperback published by
POCKET BOOKS, a division of Simon & Schuster Inc.
1230 Avenue of the Americas, New York, NY 10020

Copyright © 1991 by Parachute Press, Inc.

All rights reserved, including the right to reproduce this book or portions thereof in any form whatsoever. For information address Pocket Books, 1230 Avenue of the Americas, New York, NY 10020

ISBN: 0-671-72920-9

First Archway Paperback printing May 1991

15 14 13 12 11 10 9

FEAR STREET is a trademark of Parachute Press, Inc.

AN ARCHWAY PAPERBACK and colophon are registered trademarks of Simon & Schuster Inc.

Cover art by Bill Schmidt

Printed in the U.S.A.

IL 6+

Party
Summer

PART ONE

SUMMER PLANS

Chapter 1

A GHOSTLY PRESENCE

Sheets of rain thundered down onto the roof, a steady drumroll. The gusting wind forced a slender tree branch to click against the attic window, *tap tap tap,* like bony fingers trying to get in. Somewhere in the distance a siren wailed, its shrillness muffled by the heavy curtain of rain.

Jan closed her eyes and tried to shut out all sound.

No distractions, she thought, sweeping her black hair over her shoulder with a quick motion of her head.

Go away, world. Go away.

Eyes closed, her features tightened into an expression of intense concentration, she forced the sounds from her mind. The roar of the rain became a gentle hum and then disappeared completely. The wind slowed, then hushed. The siren vanished into the distance.

Go away, world. Go away.

On her knees on the attic floor, Jan was assaulted by a sour, musty smell—a mixture of mildew, old newspapers, dampness, and dust. It invaded her nose, caught in her throat.

I've got to shut out the smells too, she thought, holding her breath.

I've got to shut out everything, clear my mind, and concentrate. . . .

Downstairs, the dog was barking. Excited, high-pitched yips.

Jan opened her large dark eyes, then rolled them in disgust. "Can't they keep that mutt quiet?"

Foxy would be angry at me for calling him a mutt, she thought, a smile forcing its way across her serious face.

She waited for the dog to stop yipping, heard a door slam, heard the phone ring. Once. Twice.

Is anyone down there? Is anyone going to answer it?

The attic floor creaked. The rain continued to pound on the roof just above her head. She could hear the splash of water overflowing the gutter. Jan glanced back over her shoulder toward the attic steps.

Amazing how much you can hear, even with the attic door closed, she thought. Amazing how hard it is to shut out the world, even when you really try.

She turned back, squatting on her knees, and set her features, concentrating with renewed dedication. Leaning forward, she reached out and allowed her hand to trace the outlines of the pentacle she had drawn in white chalk on the wooden attic

4

floorboards. First the five-pointed star. Then the circle around the star.

The wood felt warm beneath her fingers. She ran her hand along the circle again. Again.

The light from the window dimmed. She looked up at a green-gray sky, heavy and near. A ghostly sky, she thought.

A very promising sky.

The floor beneath her seemed to grow even warmer. She stared at the pea-soup sky until she felt absorbed by it, lost in it. Everything became a green-gray, shadowless blur.

Then she shut her eyes.

The roar of the rain began to fade.

The fingers ceased their tapping against the dusty windowpane.

Go away, world. Go away.

Jan concentrated hard, remembering the instructions she had read, all of the books she had practically memorized, remembering all of the accounts she had spent so many hours poring over, absorbing, studying until she was ready.

Ready for her own encounter.

Her hand continued to trace the chalked circle and star, slowly at first, then faster, until the floor burned her fingertips.

Faster, faster. The floor was heating up now. The circle, a chalky smear, seemed to raise up beneath her fingers.

Yes, yes.

The world was gone. The heavy, noisy world was far away.

The spirit world was moving closer.

Jan could feel it, feel it under her fingertips as they circled the floor, growing hot, hot, hotter until they weren't part of her any longer. Until she wasn't part of her own fingers. Until she wasn't part of the world. Until she was no longer on her knees on the attic floor, no longer in her house. No longer anywhere.

The spirit was so close to her now.

The spirit she had summoned from the other side.

A chill ran down the length of her body, making her shudder.

Success. It was working.

She knew it was working.

She could feel the ghostly presence. She could feel it hovering over her, circling her like a dark, silent hawk.

She could feel its warmth now as it moved closer.

Yes. Yes. Yes.

She could definitely feel the presence, sense it without seeing it, feel that it was watching her, preparing to make contact.

The spirit was behind her now. She could feel the heat on her back, feel her dark hair tingle with electricity.

"I know you're here," Jan said, her voice a whisper, a tremor of sound. "I know you're here."

Silence.

Too excited to breathe, dizzy with the power she had summoned, Jan opened her eyes.

Slowly, expectantly, she turned her head.

"What are *you* doing here?" she cried.

Chapter 2

"YOU COULD GET HURT...."

Cari stood on the top attic step, her mouth hanging open in surprise and confusion. Eric laughed and slapped Craig's hand in a high-five.

"What are you doing here?" Jan repeated angrily, scrambling up from her position on the floor, violently dusting off her jeans with both hands. She tossed back her black hair, her dark eyes flashing at her three friends.

Cari, Eric, and Craig made no attempt to move from the steps. At first Cari had been startled by the scene she and the two boys had found in the attic. And now she was startled by Jan's angry reaction at being discovered.

"I didn't know you were a witch," Craig said, his expression blank, not revealing whether he was joking or not.

Eric laughed uncomfortably. "Of *course* we

knew," he joked. "Couldn't you tell from those pointy hats she always wears?"

"I thought those fit her head," Craig replied, and the two of them burst out in loud laughter that echoed through the low, narrow attic.

"You're not funny," Jan said, and her expression turned from anger to hurt. "You had no business sneaking up here and . . . and spying on me." Her voice trembled with emotion, and her eyes blinked as if holding back tears.

"I'm sorry," Cari said, finally snapping out of her trance. "Really, Jan. We didn't know. Your mom said you were up here."

"That's right," Eric said quickly, tugging at his short ponytail. "We asked her if it was okay to come up, and she said yes."

A burst of wind lashed the house. The attic window rattled, and the tree limb slammed against it hard.

Startled by the sound, all four teenagers looked to the window.

When Cari peered at Jan again, she saw that her friend had gotten herself together. "I . . . I didn't hear you come up," Jan said, pulling nervously at a strand of hair, curling it in a corkscrew around her finger.

"I don't know how you missed us. Those stairs creak like crazy," Craig said.

"Yeah. We made a lot of noise," Cari added. She moved off the step and moved toward Jan, ducking her head under the low eaves.

"I was concentrating," Jan said, glancing down

at the smeared chalk pentacle on the floor and frowning.

"We won't tell anyone you've gone crazy," Eric said, grinning.

"I *haven't* gone crazy," Jan snapped, her anger returning. "It almost worked. It *would've* worked if you hadn't—"

"What almost worked?" Cari asked, lowering herself onto the cushioned window seat in front of the rattling attic window and tucking her slender legs under her.

"Never mind," Jan muttered.

"No. Really," Cari insisted. "What were you doing?"

"You just want to laugh at me," Jan said, crossing her arms over her chest and staring out at the rain.

"We won't laugh. Promise," Eric said, glancing at Craig.

"Promise," Craig repeated obediently.

"I was summoning a ghost," Jan told them.

Eric and Craig burst out laughing.

"Come on, guys!" Cari pleaded.

Jan ignored them and faced Cari. "So what are you three doing here anyway?"

"We came to tell you we can go," Cari replied.

"To Piney Island?" Jan asked, her dark eyes glowing in the gray light from the window.

"Yeah," Cari said. "Do you believe it? My parents actually agreed."

"That's great!" Jan cried excitedly, momentarily forgetting her anger. "My aunt Rose will be so happy. I'll have to call and tell her right away." She turned back to the two boys on the stairs. "But maybe you shouldn't go."

"Huh?" Craig asked.

"What do you mean?" Eric demanded, equally surprised.

"Well, those old New England inns are all haunted, you know," Jan said.

"So?" Eric asked, leaning on Craig's shoulder.

"We don't believe in that stuff," Craig said, grinning and staring down at the smeared remains of Jan's pentacle on the floor.

"That's what I mean," Jan said, her expression almost threatening. "Ghosts in old inns usually have stories to tell. Violent stories. Bloody stories. And they don't like to be laughed at."

Her eyes burned into Eric's as she said those words. He lowered his to stare at his shoes.

"You mean—" Craig started uncertainly.

"I mean you could get hurt," Jan said heatedly. "If you laugh at them the way you laughed at me, you could get hurt."

Cari shivered and jumped up from the window seat. Despite the steamy heat of the attic, something about Jan's tone made Cari feel cold all over.

Chapter 3

EVEN THE BEST MADE PLANS . . .

Cari couldn't believe the day had actually arrived.

It hadn't been easy to get her parents to agree to let her go away for the summer. Mr. and Mrs. Taylor were overly protective of their daughter, at least that was what Cari believed.

"We just like to have you around," her father said. "You brighten up the house."

"Get real," Cari replied, making a face.

He was always saying embarrassing things like that.

"Cari has eyes as blue as the ocean on a sunny day," he would say. Or: "Cari's hair is as soft and golden as spring sunlight."

"Dad—give me a break!" she would scream.

Why does he say such stupid things? she wondered. For, despite the fact that she was as willowy and beautiful as any model on the cover of *Sassy* or

Seventeen, Cari wasn't terribly impressed with her looks.

I'm much too skinny, she sometimes thought. Or: My smile is crooked. Or: I'm so tired of wearing my hair straight back like this. I wish it wasn't so fine.

When guys at school made a fuss over her, or when they acted especially shy around her, Cari never thought it was because of her looks. She always thought it was because guys just acted that way. Basically like jerks.

Even though she was sixteen, she had never had a boyfriend, hadn't gone out on many dates without other kids around, had never even had a guy she was seriously interested in. A few crushes, that was all.

"The boys are afraid of you," her father said, unable to suppress a proud smile. "You're too beautiful."

"What planet are *you* from?" Cari had cracked, making an ugly face. She really wished he'd stop making comments like that.

Jan is the beautiful one, Cari thought. Her best friend was dark and mysterious looking, with cascading curly black hair, sparkling olive eyes, high cheekbones, full, dramatic lips, and a womanly body that made Cari feel like a stick.

Next to Jan, I'm so pale, so washed-out, I almost disappear, Cari thought. She quickly finished brushing her hair and stepped away from the mirror. She straightened her peach-colored, long-sleeved T-shirt, brushed off her white tennis shorts, and was heading down the stairs when the front doorbell rang.

"They're here!" Cari's younger sister, Lauren, called.

"Where's your suitcase?" Mr. Taylor shouted. He passed her on the stairway, acting almost frantic. "Are you packed? Are you ready?"

Cari laughed. "Yes. I'm ready. Isn't anybody going to open the door?"

"Did you remember your toothbrush?" Her mother appeared at the bottom of the stairs, looking almost as frazzled as Mr. Taylor.

"The door!" Cari insisted. "Somebody open the door!"

She pushed past her father and beat her mother to the door; her sneakers squeaked on the tile floor as she pulled it open.

"Hi," Jan said, giving Cari a look that said, "What's going on in there?"

"You must be Jan's Aunt Rose," Cari said to the attractive, middle-aged woman next to Jan. She held the screen door open, and noticed that it was a bright, clear June day, so bright that even Fear Street looked summery and cheerful.

"Nice to finally meet you," Rose said, stepping inside and shaking Cari's hand vigorously. She was wearing white slacks and a white, short-sleeved cotton sweater, which emphasized how tan she was. She had dark, curly hair like Jan's, only not as long.

"We've talked on the phone so much and Jan has told me so much about you, I feel I already know

13

you," Rose said pleasantly. Then she added, "I just didn't know you were so beautiful!"

Cari felt herself start to blush. She didn't have a chance to reply. Her father had gotten her suitcase and was dragging it into the hallway. The whole family was excitedly talking at once.

"Only one suitcase?" Jan asked Cari, surprised. "I brought a suitcase that big for my makeup!"

Cari didn't laugh. Knowing Jan, that was probably not an exaggeration! Jan was wearing a chartreuse midriff top that really emphasized her figure and skintight, white spandex bicycle shorts.

Well, Jan was never the most subtle person in the world, Cari thought. But that was what Cari liked most about her. She was bold. She didn't hold back as Cari did.

Weeks before, when her aunt had first suggested that Jan and some friends go to work at Piney Island, Jan had immediately said what she thought the point of the summer would be—to meet great new guys and to party, party, party. "It's going to be a party summer." That was Jan's phrase.

Then she invited Eric and Craig, her two oldest "boy" friends to come too, and the two guys picked up on her idea right away. "Party summer!" they repeated enthusiastically. Cari couldn't help but notice that Eric was staring at her when he said it.

The phrase had repeated itself in Cari's mind ever since.

Party summer . . .

And now she was actually leaving, after so many long arguments with her parents.

"Spend the summer working at a big New England resort hotel by yourself?" Mrs. Taylor had seemed absolutely shocked by the idea.

"I'll go too," Lauren had quickly volunteered. "Then she won't be alone."

"You keep out of it," Mr. Taylor said sharply to Lauren.

"Uh-oh. Here we go again," Cari said, frowning. "Family Argument Number 224 for the month!"

"You're keeping count?" Cari's mother cracked. "I didn't know you could count that high." She had the same wry sense of humor as Cari, which, naturally, drove Cari crazy.

"It's not an argument. It's a discussion," Mr. Taylor insisted.

"But I don't want to discuss it. I want to *do* it," Cari said impatiently, her blue eyes flashing with anger.

"Me too!" Lauren declared.

"You weren't invited," Mrs. Taylor said quietly. She turned to Cari. "Sit down, will you? Or if you're going to pace back and forth like that, carry a broom and sweep the floor. You know, make yourself useful."

"Very funny, Mom." Cari made a face, but pulled out a chair and joined them at the kitchen table.

"Now spell this out again," Mrs. Taylor said, folding her hands in front of her on the yellow Formica table. "Who all is going?"

"Well," said Cari, taking a deep breath and starting all over again, "Jan is going, and she's asked me, and Eric Bishop, and Craig Sethridge."

"He's a nice boy," Mrs. Taylor said quietly. "But isn't Eric the one with the ponytail?"

"Mom!" Cari groaned, rolling her eyes.

"And the four of you are going to work at this hotel on some island for the summer?" Mr. Taylor asked, sounding confused.

"It's not like we're going to Jupiter, Dad," Cari snapped. "And we're not going alone. Jan's aunt Rose will be there. She's a writer and needs someplace quiet to finish her book. And if I get to go and work there, I can use the pool and the beach on my time off."

"Your mother and I used to go to Cape Cod all the time," Mr. Taylor said thoughtfully. "But I never heard of this hotel."

"The Howling Wolf Inn," Mrs. Taylor said, shaking her head. "What a name. Sounds like it's out of an old horror movie or something."

"It's supposed to be really fancy and exclusive," Cari said defensively. "I guess that's why you two never heard of it!"

"Score one for Daughter Number One," said Mr. Taylor, laughing and making an invisible mark in the air.

"The inn is on a tiny, private island," Cari continued. "Piney Island. There's nothing on the island but the hotel. And the only way to reach it is by boat from Provincetown once a day. Jan says her aunt showed her pictures of it, and it's beautiful. Pine trees grow almost all the way down to the beach."

"Maybe we'll all go!" Mrs. Taylor joked.

Cari made a disgusted face.

"I want to go swimming!" Lauren cried.

"Lauren, can ι you go play or something?" Cari snapped.

"No. I want to argue too," Lauren insisted, rubbing a dirty finger across the Formica table and studying the smudge she made. "And I want to go swimming."

"Not tonight," Mrs. Taylor told Lauren. "It's almost your bedtime."

"And this is really how you want to spend your summer, working and waiting on tables in a big, drafty old hotel?" Mr. Taylor asked Cari, scratching his head.

"Yes. And having fun," Cari said, seeing that her parents were beginning to weaken. "And meeting new people. And learning new things. And swimming and vegging out on the beach. And being with my friends. And—"

"Sounds like that's what she wants," Mrs. Taylor said to her husband. "I guess it does sound better than working at the Sizzler and going to the Shadyside Swim Club on weekends."

"Well, let's give Jan's aunt a call and get the details," Mr. Taylor said. He smiled at Cari. He liked giving in to her. He liked giving her everything she wanted.

She had counted on that.

Now here it was, four weeks later. And they were cramming Cari's bag in the back of Rose's station wagon. There were hugs all around. And a few tears, mainly from Cari's mother, who still didn't like the idea of Cari being away for so many weeks. And then more goodbyes. And finally more assur-

17

ances from Rose that she'd keep a close eye on them.

Then they were pulling Lauren out of the back-seat of the station wagon. And then the weighted-down car was bumping down the Taylors' driveway. And Cari was waving to her family, saying a silent goodbye to them, to Fear Street, and to the boring summer she might have had.

Both boys were waiting at Eric's house, a rambling ranch-style house in the better section of Shadyside known as North Hills. Eric, as usual, wasn't quite ready. Half of his clothes, consisting of faded denim cutoffs and heavy-metal T-shirts, were still stacked in the living room. As Craig, Cari, and Jan looked on, Eric frantically stuffed things into a canvas bag, which was much too small to hold everything.

"My Walkman! Where's my Walkman?" Eric cried wildly, searching the room with his eyes as he continued to shove clothes into his bag.

"It's around your neck," Craig said softly, making a face.

"Oh. Of course. Where else?"

Everyone laughed.

"Hey—what's that around *your* neck?" Eric asked Jan.

Jan fingered the large white pendant she wore on a silver chain. "Nothing. Just an ivory skull. It's supposed to ward off evil." She pushed the skull toward him. "So stay away!"

"Oh, brother." Eric rolled his eyes. "You're definitely weird, Jan. You really think this hotel is going to be haunted, don't you?"

"I'll be *very* disappointed if it isn't!" Jan admitted.

Shaking his head, Eric finally managed to jam everything into his bag and zip it. Craig, of course, had packed the night before and had brought all of his stuff over to Eric's to save Rose from having to make another stop.

The two boys are as different from each other as Jan and I are, Cari thought, watching them load their stuff into Rose's station wagon. They even looked different.

Eric was short and thin. He wore an oversize yellow and red Hawaiian shirt over Day-Glo orange baggies. His dark brown hair was pulled back into a short ponytail. He had a diamond stud in one ear and wore silver wire-rimmed glasses.

He's a really nice guy, Cari thought. But he works so hard at being cool. She had always been a little attracted to Eric. They had been pretty good friends since junior high, but they'd never gone out.

Craig was more casual than cool. He kept his blond-brown hair short and neatly parted on the side. He was always dressed nicely, very preppy, that day in khaki, cuffed cotton shorts and white tennis shirt, but Cari had the feeling that Craig never gave much thought to what he wore.

He's so easygoing. He sort of floats through everything, Cari thought. In a way, she envied him. He probably never got cold sweaty hands, or that heavy feeling of dread Cari often had before a test or a first date.

By the time they finished loading, they had luggage stacked to the ceiling of the station wagon and two bags had to be strapped to the roof. "We'd better get going," Rose said, studying her watch. "Summer is almost over!"

They piled into the wagon, Jan in front beside her aunt, the two boys in back with Cari squeezed in the middle. "It's so heavy in back, the front wheels are going to fly up in the air," Jan said, turning back to look at Cari.

"Cool!" declared Eric.

"Do you have enough room back there?" Rose asked, starting the car.

"Enough room to do what?" Cari asked mischievously.

Everyone laughed.

"I've heard about your sense of humor," Rose said, backing blindly down the drive since there was no way to see out the back window.

"Does Cari have a sense of humor?" Craig teased.

"Hey—we're on our way!" Eric shouted, rolling down his window. "Goodbye, Shadyside," he shouted. "Party summer—here we come!"

"Party summer!" Craig and Cari repeated happily.

"Wait till you see the beach," Rose said, turning onto River Road, which headed out of town along the Conononka River. "I haven't been there since I was your age—"

"Five years ago?" Craig interrupted.

"Aren't you a sweetheart!" Rose said, laughing. "It was a little longer than that, but I still remember the beach. It had the softest, whitest sand I'd ever seen. And there's a sandbar a short distance from the island that keeps the ocean waves low and gentle. Perfect for swimming."

"But I brought my surfboard!" Eric protested.

"For sure, dude. Gnarly," Cari said, doing her best California airhead impression.

"Gnarlatious!" Craig added.

"You can probably surf on the other side of the island," Rose said. "The island is quite small, remember."

"I hope it's big enough to hold all the really fabulous babes I'm going to meet!" Eric said.

"Guess Eric'll be hanging out around the pool all day," Craig said.

"Yeah. Maybe I can be recreation director, or something," Eric said, grinning.

"Recreation director? Is that what they call it these days?" Jan asked, rolling her eyes.

"Tell us more about the hotel, Rose," Cari said, changing the subject.

"Yeah. How'd it get that name? The Howling Wolf Inn," Jan asked, turning around to face the front and adjusting her seat belt.

"I don't know," Rose said, turning onto the expressway, the station wagon hesitating under all the weight. "We'll have to ask Simon when we get there. I just remember that it's very big. It sprawls out in all directions. And it's very beautiful. I remember an enchanting outdoor terrace in the back by the swimming pool."

"And lots of fabulous babes," Eric said.

"Eric, give us a break," Cari pleaded.

"You guys *will* have to put in a few hours working, you know," Rose scolded.

21

"Party summer!" Craig cried.

"Party summer!" Eric took up the refrain.

As the miles rolled by, they talked about the hotel, the island, the beach, and all the things they planned to do and all the new kids they hoped to meet. Cari realized that she had never been this excited, never looked forward this much to any summer.

Here she was, away for two whole months, away from her family, on her own with her best friends, heading to a beautiful, luxurious island resort hotel.

Her friends seemed as happy and excited as she was. They rolled toward the Cape, the windows down, the radio blaring, singing along, laughing and talking the whole way.

This is *already* a great summer! Cari thought.

Their happiness didn't fade until they were on the Cape halfway between Wellfleet and Province-town, and Aunt Rose suddenly fell ill.

22

Chapter 4

A CHANGE OF PLANS

"O w!"

The station wagon swerved to the right, bumping onto the narrow shoulder of the road.

"Aunt Rose—what's wrong?" Jan cried, leaning toward her aunt, a worried expression on her face.

"My stomach—" Rose groaned.

She tried to pull the car off the narrow road, but there really wasn't room. "Ohh. What a pain!" She slowed to about thirty-five, somehow managing to keep the car on the road.

"There's got to be a place to pull over," Jan said, staring out her side of the windshield.

"What's wrong?" Cari asked.

Everyone had gotten silent. Jan reached over and clicked off the radio.

"Ohh," Rose groaned, holding her left side. "Such a sharp pain. It just came up. All of a sudden." She groaned again, but forced herself to hold the car steady, both of her hands gripping the top of the wheel.

"Never had pain like this," she said.

"Pull over. There's a field," Jan said, pointing, her voice trembling.

Rose pulled the car off the road, stopping just in front of a Route 6 sign, and shifted into Park. "Maybe if I stand up, walk around," she said, grimacing from the pain in her side. Her face, Cari saw, was white as cake flour, and a heavy sweat had broken out on her forehead.

Rose pushed open her car door. The others climbed out to help her. The narrow roadway was jammed with cars, most of them loaded down with suitcases, bicycles, boogie boards, every sort of summer equipment.

"Everyone's in a hurry to start vacationing," Rose said, leaning against the fender.

"Feel any better?" Craig asked.

"Not really." She forced a smile, but was obviously extremely uncomfortable.

"I'll drive," Jan told her.

"When did you get your license?" Rose asked, catching her breath.

"Last week," Jan admitted. "But I can do it. We should get you to a hospital."

"No!" Rose shouted, her eyes filled with fear. "No hospital."

"But, Rose," Jan pleaded, "you look really sick."

"It—it's just a pain," Rose insisted. "Ouch!" She gripped her side.

24

"Is that the appendix side?" Eric asked.

"No. The appendix is on the right," Cari told him quietly.

"She might be having a heart attack," Craig whispered, suddenly very worried. "Does the pain go down your left arm?" he asked, walking over to Rose.

"No. It's in my stomach and on my side," Rose said through clenched teeth.

Two motorcycles roared by, followed by an enormous beer truck.

"Let's find a doctor or a hospital," Jan said, trying to pull her aunt around to the passenger side. "It isn't safe here by the side of the road."

"No. No hospital. I don't believe in hospitals," Rose said, pulling out of Jan's grasp. "No doctors. Take me to Aileen."

"Aunt Aileen?"

"Yes. My sister. She's a nurse," Rose said, wiping the big drops of perspiration off her forehead with the back of her hand. "Aileen has a house just before Provincetown on Shore Road. Take me there. I'll rest up, then I'll be okay."

Jan and Craig helped Rose into the front passenger seat. She lay her head back and closed her eyes. Then Jan got behind the wheel, and Craig joined Eric and Cari in the backseat.

"When does the launch leave Provincetown for Piney Island?" Eric asked.

"Not until six this evening," Rose said, her voice sounding weak and strained. "Don't worry. I'll be fine by then."

"You don't look fine now," Jan said grimly, glancing at her aunt as she started up the station wagon. "Why are you shaking like that?"

"Chills," her aunt said. "I'll be fine. Really. Aileen's house is only a few minutes away."

"Is someone going to let me back on the highway?" Jan asked impatiently, unable to hide the tension in her voice as car after car rolled by in a steady, nonending stream.

The small road was choked with cars. It took nearly forty-five minutes to reach Aileen's house, a large, gray-shingled, barnlike structure on a hill overlooking the bay. Jan pulled the station wagon up the gravel drive and parked beside a small wooden toolshed in the back.

A few minutes ago we were all so happy, Cari thought. And now . . .

She climbed out of the car and hurried to help Rose across the tall grass to the house. "Are you feeling any better, Rose?" Cari asked.

"Not really," Rose said, even paler. Her lips were white now.

"Anybody home?" Jan called. "Aileen? Are you home?"

The back door was open, but there was no one in sight.

The sun dipped behind a large black cloud and the air suddenly grew cool. Cari could smell salt in the air. Somewhere nearby a woodpecker was tapping out a loud rhythm on a tree.

Suddenly a large woman appeared in the doorway. "Aunt Aileen!" Jan cried. Aileen, dark and exotic like Rose and Jan, pushed open the screen door and came bounding out to greet them, surprise on her face.

A few minutes later Rose was lying on the maroon leather couch in the front room, feeling a little better. Aileen was scurrying about in the small kitchen, making snacks and iced tea for everyone.

After the snacks, Cari and her friends went down to look at the bay, which was brown with grasses shooting up above the surface. "Low tide," Jan said quietly. "It's about a foot or two deep all the way out to there," she said, pointing out about half a mile.

Cari wasn't very interested in the bay. She kept checking her watch, wondering if Rose was going to recover in time for them to get into Provincetown to catch the launch for Piney Island.

The launch, Cari remembered, made the trip from Provincetown to Piney Island and back to Provincetown only once a day. If they missed the one this afternoon . . .

At five-thirty they were all gathered glumly in the front room of the old rambling beach house. Rose, who had steadfastly refused to let Aileen call a doctor, was still lying on the couch. "I'm feeling a lot better," she said, but then grabbed her side in pain.

"It's getting late," Aileen said, glancing at the copper sunburst clock above the fireplace.

"Look—you've got just enough time to get to Provincetown and make the launch," Rose said, shifting her position on the couch. "You go on without me. I'll call Simon and explain."

"What?" Jan cried, startled by the idea. Cari saw

27

that Eric and Craig were just as surprised. The idea had never occurred to any of them.

"Take the launch without me," Rose said, her voice just above a whisper. "Get settled in. Simon will take good care of you. And he needs you to start work. I don't think it's right to let him down."

"But what about you?" Jan asked.

"I'll be fine," Rose said, forcing a smile. "I'll spend some time with Aileen. I haven't seen her in months. Then I'll take the launch tomorrow and join you."

Everyone suddenly started talking at once. Jan didn't want to leave Rose. Cari tried to reassure Jan. Craig and Eric thought it was a great idea to go on without her. But finally Aileen was able to assure Jan that she would take care of Rose.

Then, after lengthy farewells, they bundled into the station wagon and Aileen drove them through Provincetown, the narrow main street crowded with tourists, to the launch slip. A handmade sign on a pole at the end of the dock said: PINEY ISLAND TOURS.

"Are you my passengers?" asked a smiling young man who appeared on the deck of the small boat and reached up for their bags. He had short, spiky blond hair, and was wearing a BOSTON U sweatshirt and white shorts.

"I guess we are," Jan said, struggling to hand him her two big suitcases. Cari and the two boys moved forward, sliding their bags along the narrow wooden dock. The gray-green ocean lapped gently at the pilings. The small boat rocked easily in the water.

Behind them, sea gulls clamored on the sand, pecking at garbage.

A few minutes later, their bags stowed in the cabin below, the four friends said goodbye to Aileen and took seats on the bench along the deck.

The young man untied the line holding the launch to the dock, and the boat began to pull away from the slip, its engine roaring loudly.

Cari leaned back against the cabin wall. The wet spray off the water felt cool and refreshing. The little boat lurched forward suddenly, throwing them all off balance, causing them to slide back and forth in their seats.

They all laughed, nervous laughter.

"We're on our own!" Eric shouted above the roar of the engine, checking out Cari as he said it.

"Party summer!" Craig yelled.

Cari laughed. She realized she was excited, and nervous, and happy, and worried—all at the same time. She felt strange about heading off to an island resort on her own, without an adult. Her parents, she knew, would have a fit!

But it was also very exciting.

Besides, what could happen?

Chapter 5

AN UNUSUAL WELCOME

"Sorry about the bumpy ride," the young man said, helping Cari onto the dock. "The water isn't usually this choppy."

"How'd we get so lucky?" Cari asked dryly, still feeling the rocking and lurching of the boat as she planted her feet on the wooden dock.

"It was great!" Craig exclaimed. "Better than any ride at Six Flags!"

"I'm soaked," Jan complained, dragging a suitcase onto the dock.

Craig helped the driver carry off the other bags.

Cari scanned the area. "There's no one here," she said, brushing her hair back behind her ears. It felt salty and wet. Her T-shirt, also soaked, clung uncomfortably to her skin.

"Rose said Simon would send someone from the hotel to pick us up," Jan said, concerned. "I don't understand. Do you think she forgot to call and say we were on our way?"

A sudden gust of wind swirled up the sand on both sides of the dock.

"I guess they're just late," Eric said, sitting down on his canvas bag.

"It's a real pretty island," the launch driver said.

Cari looked around. He was right. In the early evening light, it was so beautiful, it didn't seem real. The ocean sparkled, reflecting the rose color of the sky, crashing rhythmically against the sand, now patterned with long blue shadows. The beach stretched away from the dock on both sides of the length of the island.

A narrow road led up from the dock, winding into the tall pine trees, which stretched up, up, up a steeply sloping hill as far as they could see.

"Where's the hotel?" Cari asked.

The launch driver heaved the last of the bags onto the dock with a quiet groan. He wiped his forehead with the sleeve of his T-shirt. "Up there," he said, pointing to the trees.

"Through the trees?" Cari asked, feeling nervous.

"Yeah. You follow the road." He started to untie the rope. "You go by a gatehouse. The hotel is all fenced in. Then you just keep following the road up. You can't miss it."

He dropped the line onto the deck and pulled the launch quickly away from the dock, as if he were eager to leave.

"Is there a shuttle bus or something?" Eric asked, looking toward the trees.

But the launch was too far away, its engine grinding noisily. The driver waved once, then roared away without a backward glance.

"Where is everyone?" Craig asked, picking up his bag, then dropping it back onto the dock.

"Maybe they forgot about us," Jan said.

"Guess we'll have to walk," Cari said.

"How come we were the only ones on the boat?" Eric asked, tugging at his ponytail. "Where are all the other people who're staying at the hotel?"

"Some welcome!" Craig mumbled, staring up the road beyond the dock.

"It felt as if the ocean was pushing against us," Jan said, her face suddenly in shadow. "I kept thinking it was pushing us away, trying to keep us from coming here."

"Ooooooooooo," wailed Eric.

"Stop it," Cari pleaded. "You're giving me the creeps."

"Well, first Aunt Rose gets sick. Then the ocean gets rough and pushes against us. These are bad omens," Jan insisted, nervously fingering the skull pendant around her neck.

"Can't you forget about omens and ghosts and goblins for once?" Craig asked. "It's summer—not Halloween."

"Yeah. Give us a break," Eric muttered.

"Look, Eric, it's just a hobby of mine," Jan said. "Like your hobby is picking your nose."

"Like *your* hobby is being a total gross-out" was Eric's reply.

"Chill out, guys," Craig said unhappily.

Cari had to smile. Craig was so straight and

preppy looking, it somehow never seemed right when he tried to sound cool.

"Are we going to start walking or are we going to wait for Eric's shuttle bus?" Cari asked.

Jan laughed. "Why don't we just hail a taxi, Eric?"

"Why is everybody picking on *me?*" Eric asked in a little-boy voice.

"It's probably not a long walk," Cari said, picking up her bag. "Your aunt said the island is very tiny."

"But she didn't say it was all uphill!" Jan exclaimed, groaning as she hoisted up her two bags.

Eric swung his canvas bag over his shoulder. He tried to adjust it, but the strap had become caught in his ponytail.

He tries so hard to be cool, Cari thought. But it doesn't always work for him. But he is kind of cute anyway.

He grinned at her, as if reading her thoughts.

The four of them walked off the dock, onto the road, and into the shadows of the trees.

"Party summer!" Eric muttered under his breath.

"Stop complaining," Jan said. "We're here, aren't we? We're not hanging around in Shadyside, wondering what to do tonight, hanging out at Cari's house, wondering which movie we've seen forty times to rent again."

"Yeah, Jan's right," Cari quickly agreed, picking up the pace as they followed the road up. "We're here. We're not in Shadyside. And there are no parents around, no one to tell us what to do and—"

"I hope Aunt Rose is okay," Jan interrupted.

"You can call as soon as we get to the hotel," Cari said.

A stone gatehouse loomed into view. Behind it, a tall wrought-iron fence enclosed the hotel grounds. They walked up to the gatehouse, which was deserted, and read the green and white sign on the fence: HOWLING WOLF INN. PRIVATE PROPERTY.

"If the gate is locked, we're in trouble," Craig said.

"Don't be ridiculous," Jan said. "The gate won't be locked." Her words were positive, but her voice revealed her nervousness.

"Only one way to find out," Eric said. He gave the gate a push.

It didn't budge.

"Turn that handle there," Craig said, pointing.

"Right," Eric said. "The handle. Why didn't I think of that?"

He turned the handle and pushed.

The gate still didn't budge.

"It must be locked," Jan said. "I knew it!" She tossed down her bags and sighed dramatically.

"Take it easy. There's a phone in the gatehouse," Cari said, peering inside. "Look. We can use it to call up to the hotel."

"Great!" Jan cried, obviously relieved.

"It's getting dark so early," Craig said, raising his eyes to the sky.

"It's just the trees," Cari said. "They're blocking the sun."

She opened the narrow glass door, stepped into the gatehouse, and picked up the phone.

"Hey—there's no dial!" she exclaimed.

Eric poked his head in. "It must be some kind of intercom phone," he said. "It's probably connected to the hotel."

"But there's no dial tone or anything," Cari said, the receiver at her ear. "Guess it's not on." She replaced the receiver and stepped out of the tiny gatehouse.

"So we're locked out," Eric said, sighing unhappily.

"Well, so what?" Cari said, a devilish look on her face. She'd had a sudden inspiration. "We'll spend the night on the beach!"

"Great! A beach party! It'll be beautiful!" Jan quickly agreed, brightening a little.

"What'll we eat?" Eric asked glumly.

"The gate's open," Craig said.

"Huh?" Cari wasn't sure she heard right.

"The gate's open," Craig repeated, a broad grin on his handsome face. "There was a latch down there," he explained, pointing. "It just had to be flipped."

He pulled open the gate.

"Let's go!" Jan cried happily, picking up her bags.

"I always said Craig was a mechanical genius," Eric exclaimed.

"I still want to spend the night on the beach," Cari said, pouting.

"We'll have the whole summer for that," Craig said brightly.

All four of them chattered enthusiastically as they made their way up the sloping hill, through the trees. Birds twittered and trilled. A tiny baby rabbit ran right across their path without stopping.

Then suddenly the Howling Wolf Inn came into view.

"How beautiful!" Cari cried.

They all stopped in the middle of the road to admire it.

It looked like a set designer's idea of a resort hotel, enormous and white with a sloping, red-shingled roof, set back on a wide, manicured lawn, two wings jutting out from a central building along the top of the hillside, a screened-in porch filled with wicker chairs and chaises, twin columns on either side of the red front doors.

As Cari and her friends drew closer, they could see the bay behind the hotel and the wooden stairs leading down to a private beach with several canoes tied to a small dock.

"All right! Get a load of that beach!" Eric cried.

"It's perfect," Cari said. "Just perfect."

"It's better than Aunt Rose described it," Jan said breathlessly.

"There's the pool," Craig said, pointing. "It's enormous. And that must be a pool house behind it."

"Where is everybody?" Cari said suddenly.

"What?" Jan asked, her eyes still surveying the majestic old hotel that seemed to stretch endlessly in front of them.

"There's no one in the pool," Cari said.

"Maybe they're all inside having dinner," Eric suggested. "I know that's where *I'd* like to be."

"But there are no lights on in the rooms," Cari

said. "There's no one on the beach. No one walking on the grounds. No one on the porch."

"Cari's right," Jan said quietly.

Cari had a sudden chill.

"The whole hotel just for us!" Craig exclaimed.

Everyone ignored his cheerful outburst.

"Come on," Jan said, leading the way up the expansive front walk onto the porch and straight to the tall, red double doors that formed the entrance. She tried to pull the doors open, but they wouldn't budge. So she rang the bell.

Cari could hear it chime somewhere deep inside the hotel.

They waited more than a minute or two. Then Jan rang the bell again.

A few seconds later the door was pushed open a few inches. A very pale, middle-aged man with unruly tufts of black hair standing up on his head and a very stern, unpleasant expression poked his head out the crack.

"Go away. Please. We're closed," he said and pulled the door shut.

Chapter 6

FEAR

"Some welcome," Cari said glumly, staring at the red door.

"Did he say they were *closed?*" Eric asked, his eyes behind the wire-rimmed glasses wide with disbelief.

"Maybe this is the wrong hotel," Craig said, grinning.

Cari gestured to the engraved bronze sign set in the shingles beside the doorway: HOWLING WOLF INN. ESTABLISHED 1853.

"For sure," she said. "There are probably two Howling Wolf Inns on this island. Let's go find the other one."

"Right. You lead the way, Craig," Eric said, rolling his eyes.

Jan, who hadn't said a word, sighed and kicked her suitcase. "I don't understand it," she said. "I

38

know that Aunt Rose arranged this very carefully. She spoke to the owner several times and—"

"But there's no one here!" Eric cried. "The place is empty. It's closed. Just like the man said."

"Wow," Craig said, shaking his head.

"That's a helpful comment," Cari cracked. Then she immediately regretted it, seeing the hurt look on Craig's face.

"He was so rude," Craig said. "I really don't believe this."

"Maybe he's building a monster down in his basement laboratory," Jan said. "He's about to bring it to life tonight, and he doesn't need four teenagers interfering with his plans."

"Ooooooooo," Eric howled a scary movie howl. "Welcome to Castle Frankenstein!"

"Give us a break," Cari said, sighing.

As Eric started to howl again, the front door was suddenly opened all the way. "Whoa!" Eric cried in surprise and stumbled down the steps off the porch.

A tall, distinguished-looking man with wavy white hair and a full white mustache stood before them in the doorway. He was wearing a khaki safari jacket over stylish, pleated white trousers. He smiled at them, and his dark eyes seemed to twinkle.

"Good evening," he said in a deep rich voice. His smile didn't fade as he looked at them as if searching for someone he knew.

Jan said hello and started to stammer out something else. But he interrupted her. "Please accept my apologies for the behavior of my servant, Martin. I am afraid that your appearance caught Martin a little off guard, and the poor man doesn't deal with surprises very well." He chuckled, a warm, conspiratorial chuckle.

"I'm a bit surprised to see you here myself," he said, staring at Jan. "Where is Rose? I understood she was coming with you."

"My aunt got sick before we reached Provincetown," Jan explained. "She told us to go on ahead. She'll come on the next launch. Didn't you speak to her?"

"You must be Jan," the man said, not answering her question. He extended a large hand and shook Jan's vigorously. "Yes. Yes. I can see the family resemblance."

"Thank you," Jan said uncertainly, finally managing to disentangle her hand from his.

"Excuse me. I'm being as rude as Martin," the man said, holding the door open wider and motioning for them to go inside. "Allow me to introduce myself. I am Simon Fear. Simon Fear the Third, to be precise. I am the owner of this humble inn."

"Simon Fear?" Cari blurted out. "I live on a street called Fear Street. Back in Shadyside. There's an old burned-out mansion down the block. It's—"

"It belonged to my great-uncle," Simon said. "A very mysterious man, as I'm sure you've heard. I haven't been back to Shadyside in many years, not since I chose to live here year-round. Has it changed much?"

"I don't think so," Cari said, not sure how to answer.

"Is everyone in the Fear Street cemetery still

dead?" Simon asked, and then he laughed heartily, throwing his head back and closing his eyes.

Cari and her friends, dragging their bags into the front hall and lobby, replied with nervous laughter.

Cari studied the lobby. It was huge but sparsely furnished, with dark wood walls and a high ceiling with exposed wooden beams. The chairs and tables, grouped along one wall and in clusters in the corners, were heavy and wintry, dark wood and plush velvet and leather cushions, not what Cari expected to find in a summer resort.

It looks more like a hunting lodge, she thought.

"Just leave your bags here," Simon Fear instructed. "Martin is probably preparing rooms for you now. When he's finished, he'll take the bags to your rooms."

"Where is everyone?" Jan asked, scanning the vast, empty lobby.

"We're closed," Simon said, pulling at his white mustache and studying her as he answered her question. "I can't believe your aunt didn't receive my letter."

"Letter?"

"Yes. The phones were out all last week. So I sent an overnight letter. Rose knew we were refurbishing the inn, redoing the dining room and some of the guest rooms in the old wing. I thought the work would all be finished by now. But in the middle of everything, the workers picked up and left. In my letter, I asked Rose if you could all come in two or three weeks when the work is finally finished and we're up and running."

"Aunt Rose must not have received the letter,"

Jan said unhappily. "So we've come all this way for nothing."

"I'll gladly put you up until the launch comes from Provincetown tomorrow evening," said Simon sympathetically. "Martin is a very good cook. And you can use the pool and the beach while you wait."

So much for our party summer, Cari thought, surprised at how miserable and disappointed she felt. So much for clambakes at night on the beach, and meeting new kids, and swimming in the ocean, and being on our own for an entire summer—and maybe meeting someone special.

"Have you eaten dinner?" Simon asked.

"No," Eric quickly replied.

Everyone laughed. Eric's reply had been so impassioned.

"Come into the dining room," Simon said, leading the way, taking long, expansive strides. "I'll ask Martin to prepare something."

Cari and Jan exchanged glances as they followed Simon Fear to the dining room. Jan looked as disappointed as Cari felt. "What a shame. This place is neat looking," Jan whispered.

Cari nodded in agreement. She checked out the boys. Eric seemed to be tense and unhappy, but Craig had his usual calm expression. He was always the same—he always seemed to float through any situation.

He *must* be disappointed too, Cari thought. Why doesn't he show it?

"Here we are," Simon said, gesturing as they entered the large, carpeted room. He flicked on several low-hanging chandeliers and the room brightened into view. Two long tables were set with tablecloths and china and silverware by the long windows across the back of the room. The rest of the tables had chairs stacked upside down on them. Scaffolding stood beside the wall to the left, a stained canvas drop cloth hanging over its side. Part of the wallpaper was peeled off behind the scaffolding, and some of the ceiling molding had been removed.

"My workers," Simon said grumpily, pointing to the torn-up wall. "They were on the job for three weeks, and then they got a call to go work on some rich psychiatrist's house in Wellfleet. So they took off. Lord knows when they'll be back."

Cari and Eric walked over to the big window that practically covered the entire back wall of the dining room. "What a view!" Cari cried.

The sun was setting. From the dining room, she could see the back terrace filled with deck furniture, tables, and umbrellas. And beyond that the hotel beach and the bay, silver-gray against the darkening sky. The water seemed to shimmer, unreal, like cartoon water, like an artist's version of what a beach scene should look like.

"Wow," Craig said, joining them.

You do have a way with words, Cari started to say, but stopped herself, remembering how her last crack had hurt Craig. Besides, *wow* was the correct word. The view was spectacularly beautiful.

"I do hope your aunt isn't terribly ill," Simon said to Jan as they all continued to admire the view, watching the evening sky.

"She was refusing to go to a doctor," Jan said. "She's so stubborn. Can I give her a call?"

"Certainly you can, tomorrow morning. The lines are fixed but the hotel switchboard is down," Simon said. "I'm afraid we can't call out. Someone is supposed to come out from the Cape to fix it tomorrow."

At that moment Martin entered the room, coughing loudly, wiping his mouth with a white linen handkerchief. Everyone turned away from the window to look at him.

He was short and thin, and wore a starched, short-sleeved white shirt over black trousers. His black hair was tousled and standing out at the sides as if he had forgotten to brush it. He had a lean face with small gray eyes set close together over a long, pointed nose. His mouth was set in a straight line as if he disapproved of everything he saw.

"This is Martin," Simon said, smiling. "I believe you met him . . . briefly." Simon laughed heartily again.

Martin reddened but his disapproving expression didn't change.

"Martin, our unexpected guests are hungry. What can we offer them from the kitchen?"

"There's some barbecued chicken," Martin said. His voice was thin and reedy, a contrast to Simon's deep, booming tones. "And I guess I can put together a salad." He said this grudgingly, as if it were the last thing in the world he wanted to do.

"Excellent," Simon said, ignoring Martin's attitude. He shooed Martin to the kitchen with a wave of his large hand. Martin lowered his head and walked quickly toward the double kitchen doors without glancing back.

"Come sit down," Simon said, pulling out a couple of chairs at one of the setup tables. "Let's have a nice chat. It's been so lonely here since we closed the place. I like it better when the hotel is streaming with young people."

Me too, thought Cari with some bitterness.

She took a seat with the others and studied the vast, empty dining room. It seemed so sad, this giant room with all the chairs overturned, all the tables empty. That beautiful view, that beautiful beach with no one there to appreciate it.

Maybe we can get in a few hours on the beach tomorrow before we have to go back, Cari thought.

Back.

Back to Shadyside. Back to hanging around the house. She probably wouldn't even be able to get a summer job. Most likely they were all taken by now.

"We hope to open again by the end of July," Simon was saying. "Maybe sooner, if my workers ever decide to come back. My brother Edward and I decided to do the renovation last March. We wanted to have it all finished in time for the summer tourist season. Maybe it was all a big mistake."

It was *definitely* a mistake, Cari thought. For some reason, she found herself thinking about Lauren, her little sister. Lauren will think this is really funny, Cari thought. She was so jealous that I

45

was going away for the summer. Now she'll be laughing at me for months.

Cari was feeling so sorry for herself, she barely had any appetite when Martin reappeared with the food. Her thoughts wandered. She heard only part of the conversation, and only spoke a couple of times when Simon asked her a direct question.

Simon is really charming, Cari thought. He's so warm and friendly. I like the way his black eyes sparkle in the light—they always seem to be laughing. I wonder why he puts up with that sour-faced Martin.

"My brother Edward is quite moody and depressed," Simon was saying. His expression darkened and his eyes watered over. "Quite depressed. It's really a pity. He won't come downstairs now when anyone's here. I'm doing this renovation mainly to cheer him. It was a bad business decision, but we don't really need the money. I only care about helping him. He likes projects of all kinds, so—"

"Hey, I've got a great idea!" Eric interrupted, swallowing a mouthful of barbecued chicken. "You know, Craig and I are really good in shop. We're good carpenters."

"Yeah, that's true," Craig said, forking more salad from the big wooden bowl onto his plate.

"Maybe we could stay and help with the renovation work," Eric said eagerly.

"That's a *great* idea!" Cari chimed in, immediately cheered. "Jan and I could help too."

"We could probably get a lot of it done while

46

you're waiting for your workers to return," Eric said.

"It would be fun," Jan added, "and we'd do a super job. Really!"

Simon Fear laughed. "You know . . . it might be a good idea."

"I really wouldn't advise it," a low voice said from the kitchen doors. Everyone turned to see Martin standing with a large tray in his hands. "Work like this should be done by professionals," he said sharply, disapproval showing on his face.

"It's all very simple carpentry," Simon argued. "And a little wallpaper stripping. I think they could handle it. Probably do a better job than those clowns I hired!" He laughed.

Martin didn't join in the laughter. His face remained rigid. "It isn't *safe*," he said, staring right at Cari.

Cari had a sudden chill.

Something about the way Martin said that made her feel that he wasn't concerned for their safety. He made it sound more like a *threat*.

It isn't safe.

"I really think it better if they leave on the next launch," Martin said stiffly, still holding the large, empty tray at his side.

"I'm not sure I agree. It might be good for Edward to have some young people about the place," Simon said thoughtfully, staring out the window into the now dark night.

"It would be better if they left," Martin insisted, speaking each word slowly, distinctly, as if he were talking to a child.

47

"It might be nice for *me* to have some young people here," Simon said, ignoring his servant's patronizing tone.

"There will be plenty of young people when we reopen," Martin said sharply, not bothering to conceal his impatience. "They will only be in the way now."

"We're real hard workers," Eric said to Simon.

"We'll do a good job," Craig agreed, smiling at Cari.

"Then it's settled," Simon said, giving his mustache a tug. "They will stay and help out with the carpentry work."

Cari checked to see how Martin took the news. He didn't react at all. His face became an expressionless blank. His small gray eyes seemed to glaze over. He stood rigid, then raised the tray. "May I clear?" he asked as if the disagreement between himself and his employer had never taken place.

Cari turned back to her friends, who were cheering and applauding Simon's decision, and she happily joined in the celebration. They were all excitedly talking at once until Simon raised a hand for quiet.

"Of course I don't expect you to spend all your time working," he said, grinning. "It's also required that you put in some time on the beach or at the pool. Catch some rays. I believe that's what you young people call it."

Everyone laughed.

"Party summer!" Eric and Craig cried in unison.

"Yes, yes. That's the idea. I hope you have a wonderful time at Howling Wolf. Most people do."

Smiling at them all, Simon pushed his chair back and stood up. He swept a hand back through his thick, silvery hair. "We will try to contact your aunt Rose tomorrow," he said to Jan. "I'm so disappointed that she isn't here, but I'm sure she's getting along fine."

"Aileen is a good nurse," Jan said. "But I would like to call to find out how Aunt Rose is."

"Martin, please show these young people to their rooms," Simon said.

Martin stopped collecting the dinner plates and plopped down his tray heavily, making a loud, unnecessary crash.

"Did you set them up in the new section?" Simon asked.

Martin shook his head, keeping his eyes down on the floor. "No. The old wing."

Simon's face filled with surprise. But his smile quickly returned. "Well, have a pleasant evening. I'll see you in the morning, and we will begin work."

Cari and her friends thanked Simon. Then chattering excitedly, they followed Martin through the dining room and down a dimly lit corridor, which smelled of mothballs and detergent.

This *must* be the old wing, Cari thought. It probably wouldn't look so bad if the lights were on.

Following Martin, who walked rapidly, ignoring them, his eyes focused on the carpet, they turned a corner, walked down another long corridor with closed doors on both sides, turned another corner, and continued to walk.

We've walked miles, Cari thought. Where is he taking us?

Finally Martin stopped in front of an open door. The bronze number on the door said 123-C.

"This place is bigger than it looks!" Eric declared.

Martin scowled. "I made up the next four rooms for you," he said. "You can decide who gets which room."

"Thank you," Jan said softly.

"I really don't think you should stay here," Martin said to her.

"What?"

"You heard me," he said sharply. "I don't think you should stay here. It could be dangerous."

"What?" Cari cried.

"The construction work, I mean," Martin said, staring into her eyes. "It's a lot more work than Simon realizes, and very difficult."

"Well, we're willing to work hard," Eric told him.

"I don't think you'll enjoy your stay," Martin said ominously, still staring at Cari. "This old place isn't much fun when it's empty."

"Don't worry. We'll be fine," Jan assured him.

"I'm not so sure," he said. "There are . . . other things. Things that you would be better off not knowing about." As he spoke these words, his voice faded to a whisper.

"You mean the place is *haunted?*" Jan asked eagerly. "Are there ghosts?"

Jan's questions seemed to surprise him. He gazed at her thoughtfully. He seemed to be trying to decide how much to reveal.

"I'm warning you—" he started.

"Well, *are* there?" Jan demanded. "Have you seen ghosts here?"

He was silent for a long moment. "I have seen things," he said reluctantly. "Here in the old wing."

His tone was odd, cold—almost as if he were teasing them, Cari thought.

A strange, thin-lipped smile formed on Martin's shadowy face. "You don't believe in ghosts—do you?" he whispered.

"No," both Eric and Craig exclaimed.

"Yes," Jan said. "Please—tell us what you've seen."

"Leave this place. Go back tomorrow," Martin said, ignoring her question.

His face was entirely in shadow. Cari couldn't see his expression, but his words gave her another chill.

He turned sharply and, without another word, floated silently away down the dark, empty corridor.

Chapter 7

A SURPRISE AT DINNER

"Hand me the suntan lotion," Cari said, lazily reaching up.

"Which one? The coconut one or the one that tastes like bananas?" Eric asked, sitting up to search through Cari's straw beach bag.

"I don't really care what they taste like," Cari said, laughing. She shielded her eyes with her hand to peer at Eric, who was beside her on the big yellow beach blanket, wearing faded denim cutoffs. "What number is the coconut one?"

"It's eight," Eric said, twisting off the cap and rubbing some of the white lotion onto his pale shoulders.

"Okay," said Cari. "That's good. I want to get a tan, but I don't want to roast."

Eric handed her the tube. Cari began rubbing the lotion on her arms and shoulders, still lying flat on her back.

"Where is Jan?" Cari asked.

"I don't know," Eric said. He was watching Craig, who was down by the water in lime green baggies, letting the low waves froth around his ankles.

"She wasn't at breakfast or lunch. I haven't seen her all day," Cari said, a little worried.

"She's probably off somewhere, searching for ghosts and goblins," Eric said, snickering. "Maybe she's in a deep trance, trying to summon the Ghost of the Howling Wolf Inn."

"I love Jan, but she really is weird," Cari said.

"I heard that!" a voice cried right behind Cari.

Cari sat up and spun around. Jan, wearing a pink bikini and carrying a large canvas beach bag, stood over her, an angry expression on her face.

"Jan—we were just wondering where you were," Cari said.

"I know. I heard your whole conversation," Jan said. "So you think I'm weird, huh?"

"Jan—" Cari started.

"Think I'm crazy, huh? Think my interest in the paranormal is one big joke?"

"Yeah. Kind of," Eric agreed, unable to keep a straight face.

Jan scowled at him.

"Sit down," Cari said, patting the beach blanket. She gave Eric a shove. "Move over. Make room. And stop picking on Jan." She looked up at her friend. "Come on, Jan. It's such a beautiful day. It's much too pretty to be arguing."

"I really don't like to be laughed at," Jan insisted. She grudgingly lowered herself onto the blanket.

"I'm sorry. Really," Eric said, but his grin didn't make his words too believable. He adjusted his mirrored sunglasses and gazed at the water.

"Where've you been?" Cari asked.

"Oh, I slept very late," Jan told her, pulling towels out of her enormous bag. "Then I explored a little and tried to call Aunt Rose, but there was no answer. Simon thinks she'll come out today. He's going to drive down to the dock to meet the launch later. I hope she's on it."

"Me too," Cari said quietly.

"This is a great place!" Eric exclaimed, stretching out beside Jan, who was still pulling things from her bag.

"It's okay," Jan said, concentrating on finding the suntan lotion. "Anybody ready to swim?"

"Looks like Craig is ready to go in," Eric replied. "Hey—look at that bird."

Cari and Jan followed his gaze. A large dark shape glided swiftly across the pale sky.

"It's a hawk," Jan said.

"They have hawks here?" Eric asked, still following the bird's progress, the sky reflected in the lenses of his sunglasses.

"Guess so," Cari said. The dark bird seemed out of place where everything was so bright and shiny and pretty. Cari somehow felt the bird was an intruder, an unwanted visitor casting a shadow on their private beach.

She shook away that strange thought and sat up, propping herself on one elbow after adjusting her shimmering green bikini top.

Craig was still standing at the edge of the water

with his back to them, the blue-green water sparkling with sunlight as it lapped gently onto the yellow sand. To the right, two small canoes bobbed against a low wooden dock. The bay beach rolled off on both sides of them, following the curve of the shoreline.

Behind them, up a sloping dune, the hotel stood, a sprawling, white fortress guarding the entire scene, the long dining-room window catching the gold of the afternoon sun. And on both sides, the hotel was framed by woods of fragrant, tall, blue-green pines, swaying ever so gently in the warm breeze off the water.

"I can't believe it! This is all *ours!*" Cari exclaimed, filled with happiness. "It's just so beautiful! I'm *glad* no one else is here!"

"It's not bad," Jan said, rolling onto her stomach. "Not bad at all."

"Not bad?" Cari cried. "It's *paradise!*"

"I keep waiting for Gilligan and the Skipper to come walking out from the trees," Eric said.

"Isn't that show a little sophisticated for you?" Cari cracked.

He tossed a handful of sand onto her legs.

"Hey! You're getting sand all over the blanket!" Jan protested.

"I know," Eric said, pleased with himself.

"Can't take you anywhere," Cari said, frowning.

He's cute in those mirror sunglasses and jean cutoffs, she thought. I like his ponytail too. Her thoughts surprised her. She'd never thought of Eric as anything but a friend, but now she suddenly felt attracted to him.

55

It must just be the great mood I'm in, she thought. I'm attracted to *everybody* today.

"It was nice of Simon to give us the day off to have fun," Jan said.

"He's a nice guy," Eric said. "He's a cool dude. He's so distinguished looking. Like an ambassador or something."

"Yes, it was really great of him to let us stay," Cari said thoughtfully. "But what's with this Martin character?"

"Did you see his face at breakfast? Like a stewed prune!" Eric said, laughing.

"What's his problem anyway?" Cari asked, sifting her hand through the warm sand. "Did you get the feeling he was trying to scare us last night?"

All three of them laughed.

"He wasn't very subtle," Cari said.

"He sure didn't want to tell us about the ghost," Jan said, pulling herself up onto one elbow.

"Oh, please don't start up about ghosts again," Eric pleaded.

Jan's dark features tightened in anger. "I'm tired of you making fun of me. You think you know everything, but you don't," she said sharply. "You know, this island was probably inhabited in colonial days, like three hundred fifty years ago or something. This area is very old. So many spirits have passed through here. New England is filled with old houses and inns and hotels that are inhabited with ghosts from those times. I don't think Martin was lying to us or trying to scare us last night. I think he was warning us."

"Someone should've warned us about *you!*" Eric cracked, grinning.

Jan sat up angrily. "Listen, Eric—just knock it off, okay?"

Cari knew that Jan was really upset by Eric's teasing, but Eric didn't seem to realize it. He jumped to his feet and stretched his hands out in front of him and began playfully advancing on Jan, wide-eyed, a big grin on his face, howling like a Halloween ghost. *"Ooowooooooo!"*

Jan scowled angrily, got up, and started to walk away from him. "I mean it, Eric—"

But he started to chase after her, lumbering like Frankenstein's monster, howling at the top of his lungs. Jan started to run up the dunes toward the hotel with Eric in close pursuit, laughing and howling.

Eric stopped at the edge of the sand, lowering his hands. But Jan kept going, taking long strides, her face red with anger.

"Hey, Jan—" Eric called. "Jan—come back!"

She ignored his calls and disappeared into the hotel.

"What's with her? I was just teasing," Eric said, jogging back to Cari.

Cari shrugged. "I guess she doesn't have much of a sense of humor about ghosts," she said.

"Maybe she's just stressed out about her aunt," Eric suggested, staring up at the hotel.

"Maybe," Cari replied.

"Hey—how about a swim?"

They looked down to the water and heard Craig calling to them, his hands cupped around his mouth. "Come on!" he shouted, signaling for them to join him.

"I'm ready," Eric said, whipping off his sunglasses.

He helped Cari up. His hands felt warm on her arms. She smiled at him. He didn't let go of her right away. Their eyes met. "Come on! Let's check out the water!"

That evening, under a sky streaked with scarlet, as the sun lowered behind the pine trees and a pale full moon appeared above them, the four friends found themselves back on the beach.

Eric had apologized to Jan, and she had grudgingly accepted his apology. They had changed into shorts and T-shirts. The cool evening air made their fresh sunburns tingle.

"Wow! I mean, what a sunset!" Craig exclaimed, lying back on the sand and staring up at the sky.

Cari stood next to Eric, watching the colors of the sky reflect on the water. "I feel like I'm in an enchanted place," she said.

"It's even prettier than Shadyside," Eric joked. He was standing very close to her. She smiled at him.

"Would somebody help me with this blanket?" Jan was struggling with a large striped beach blanket. Cari hurried over to help her spread it across the sand. They anchored it with the two large picnic baskets they had brought.

"I'm starving," Craig said, dropping down onto the blanket and starting to pull open the nearest basket. "What did Martin pack for us?"

"Uh . . . let me guess," Cari said. "Tuna fish sandwiches?"

"Guess again," Craig told her, pulling out an elegant platter. "Cold lobster. Wow."

"What's in this basket?" Eric asked, opening the lid. "Hey—no wonder it was so heavy. It's a big tureen of clam chowder." He lifted out the big container and then pulled out a bowl filled with salad and two long French breads still warm from the oven.

"What a feast!" Jan declared.

They pulled out the china plates, silverware, and cloth napkins Martin had packed and arranged everything on the blanket. Then they set up and lit the two candles they found at the bottom of the basket. The sky was darkening to purple as the sun sank behind the trees. The moon glowed now as they began to eat dinner, the lapping water of the bay providing soft background music for their elegant beach party.

"I feel like I'm in a movie," Jan said.

"I've never seen a movie this good!" Cari exclaimed.

Cari lifted her eyes to the hotel, which stood outlined in the darkness, just two first-floor windows lighted, like cat's eyes peering down on them from above.

"After dinner, let's take a swim," Eric suggested, a devilish grin on his face.

"We don't have our bathing suits," Craig said.

"So?" Eric replied, his grin growing wider.

"I used to have this recurring dream about swimming at night under a full moon," Cari said.

"That's a very interesting dream," Eric said.

"You should be very embarrassed," Craig added, joining in.

"Oh, shut up," Jan snapped. "You're both ridiculous."

"Oh—look!" Cari cried suddenly. She was staring up at the top of the low dune. "There's someone there!"

They all turned to see a large figure, only a shadow in the darkness, standing as still as a statue above them on the dune.

"Who *is* it?" Cari asked, suddenly filled with fear.

Chapter 8

NO BONES

The large figure stepped out of the shadow into the moonlight.

"Simon!" Jan called.

He gave them a quick wave, not moving from his place at the top of the dune. His lustrous, white linen suit shimmered and glowed in the moonlight.

He looks like a ghost, Cari found herself thinking. She was still trying to get over the shock of seeing him there, so dark and so still.

Now, with his white suit, his slicked-back white hair, and white mustache, Simon radiated light.

"Come down!" Jan called.

"Yes, join us!" Cari shouted up to him.

Simon made his way down the dune, moving with surprising agility. He stood over them, his eyes surveying the blanket. Cari saw that he was carrying a bottle of white wine and a fluted wineglass.

"Is Aunt Rose here?" Jan asked anxiously. "Was she on the launch?"

"No, I'm afraid not," Simon told her. "But don't worry. I'm sure she's fine. She must have decided to spend a little extra time with her sister in Provincetown."

"But why didn't she call?" Jan asked anxiously.

"She probably tried this morning before our phone problems were fixed. Don't worry. We shouldn't disturb her tonight—we'll let her rest. But first thing tomorrow we'll talk to her, and all will be well. I promise." Before Jan could reply, he changed the subject. "I see that Martin has provided you with a little snack," he said, surveying the remains of the elegant dinner.

Everyone laughed. "It was a little more than a snack," Cari said, motioning for him to sit down with them.

"Marta, our cook, doesn't return until Friday," Simon said, smiling. "Martin complains. But I think he enjoys having a chance to be creative in the kitchen."

"It was great, but now we're too stuffed to do any work tomorrow," Eric joked.

"Yes, I think I put on ten pounds," Cari added.

"I'll sweat it out of you in the morning. Don't worry," Simon replied. He sat down nimbly on the edge of the blanket and poured himself a glass of wine. "A toast to you all," he said, raising the glass to them before taking a long sip.

His expression suddenly turned somber. "I wish Edward had joined us," he said. "I begged him to come down, but he's being very stubborn."

"Is your brother sick?" Jan asked with a mouthful of bread.

The question seemed to surprise Simon. "Sick? No," he said thoughtfully. "He's just very depressed." He brightened a little. "We Fears can be quite moody, you know."

"We've all heard stories about your family," Cari blurted out. "I mean . . . not *your* family. But your grandparents. You know. Your ancestors, I guess."

She could feel herself blushing. It wasn't like her to be so tongue-tied.

"Cari lives very near the old Fear mansion back in Shadyside," Jan explained to Simon.

"My parents love fixing up old houses," Cari said. "I can see the old Fear mansion from my bedroom window."

Simon closed his eyes as if trying to picture it. "Yes, yes. There certainly are a lot of stories about that house. And about my family." He opened his eyes and directed his gaze across the blanket at Cari.

A soft wind swirled around them, as if trying to keep everyone there, to hold them in place.

"Was Simon Fear your grandfather?" Jan asked.

Simon took a sip of wine. "No. He was my grandfather's brother. My great-uncle."

"But you were named after him?" Jan asked.

"Not exactly." A strange, crooked smile crossed his face, which was now half-hidden in shadow. "My father's name was Simon too."

From somewhere in the pine woods an animal began to howl, a sad, mournful sound.

"Tell us about the first Simon Fear," Jan pleaded

eagerly, leaning forward on the blanket. "Please tell us about the old mansion on Fear Street. Tell us what *really* happened there."

Cari felt embarrassed. Jan was being impolite, she thought. But Simon didn't seem to mind.

"I don't really know that much," he said. "I mean, it was long before I was born. And the details, well, they're sketchy, to say the least." He looked up the sloping dune to the old hotel. "I wish Edward were here. He could tell the story better than I."

"Oh, please," Jan urged. "How did the mansion get burned down? Are all those weird stories about Simon Fear true?"

Simon chuckled and put down his wineglass. Everyone leaned forward in anticipation. The candles flickered but didn't go out.

"As I'm sure you know, Simon Fear, my great-uncle, was one of the first settlers of Shadyside," he began. "He was very rich. At least, that's the way the family has passed the story down.

"He was wealthy when he arrived in Shadyside, although no one knows where his money came from. For that matter, no one seems to know where *Simon* came from!"

"What did he look like?" Jan asked eagerly. "Do you look like him?"

Simon shrugged, the broad shoulders of his white suit jacket seeming to float up into the dark night air. "No one knows what Simon Fear looked like. There are photos from that time of the rest of our family, but there are none of him. That's another of the mysteries."

He raised his glass, took a sip of wine, licked his lips, then continued. "Another mystery was why he built his fabulous mansion so far from town. For as I'm sure you know, there was no Fear Street in those days. In fact, there were no streets *at all* in that undeveloped part of town. Simon Fear built his enormous mansion back in the woods. It was so completely secluded, it could only be reached by following a dirt path through the trees. That's the path the workers made to get to the house as they were building it."

"I guess he liked his privacy," Jan said.

"Well, he was not exactly a private man," Simon said, contradicting her. "Not at first, anyway. When he moved to Shadyside, Simon and his beautiful young wife, Angelica, were the toasts of the town. They were seen everywhere. Their mansion may have been secluded, but it is said that the lights there were always burning. Simon and Angelica threw lavish parties, and the house was always filled with guests.

"The Fears were extremely popular and well liked," Simon continued, his face orange in the flickering candlelight. "They did a lot for the town. Simon used his money to build the library, and he helped to build Shadyside's first hospital."

Simon paused to take a sip of wine. Cari glanced across the blanket at Jan, who had a disappointed expression on her face. So far, at least, this wasn't the kind of story any of them had expected.

"Simon and Angelica had two beautiful daughters," Simon went on. "Simon adored them both. Adored them too much, maybe. He didn't treat them like ordinary children. He didn't let them go to school. He brought in a tutor instead. He bought them anything and everything they wanted—and more. One year, so the story goes, he imported an entire circus from Europe—animals and all—and had them give a performance just for one of the girls' birthdays."

"That's cool," Eric said.

"Shhh. Don't interrupt," Jan said.

"It must have seemed to my great-uncle, living such a luxurious life in his secluded mansion, that the good times would go on forever," Simon said, staring out at the dark water as he continued. An ominous tone had entered his voice. "But they didn't.

"One day Simon's two little girls went out to play in the woods. They didn't return. That night and into the next morning, a frantic search ensued. The story goes that their bodies were found in the woods more than a week later. Their bodies—but not their bones. Their skeletons had been completely removed."

"Oh, yuck! That *can't* be true!" Cari gasped, suddenly filled with horror, trying to picture two little girls without their bones.

Simon shrugged, his face expressionless in the candlelight. "I'm just telling you the stories that were told to me."

"How awful! Did the police find the murderer?" Jan asked, her dark eyes wide.

"I don't know if they were invited to try," Simon said mysteriously. "After that, the lights in the large mansion in the woods never burned again. Everything changed. Angelica was never seen in town again. The story goes that she went completely mad, locked herself in her room, never came out. At night, people all the way across the woods would hear strange and terrifying howls and cries, coming, they guessed, from Angelica's room.

"And Simon? His life seemed to end as well. Simon lost all his money. Maybe he didn't lose it. Maybe he gave it away. All of the priceless paintings and sculptures in the house were sold, carted away. Simon, too, was never again seen in town. And then, mysteriously, the house burned down."

"Did Simon burn it down?" Jan asked.

"I don't really know. I don't think anyone does. Some say that Angelica, in her madness, set it aflame to punish Simon for bringing her to the place. Others say that Simon did it, bringing his house to an end along with his life. There was a written report by a man, their nearest neighbor, who happened to be in the woods. I've seen it. This person wrote that the house burst into flame and that the flames roared for hours, but the house didn't burn until much later. 'Hellfire,' he called it. After that report, few people would venture near the mansion."

Simon paused, silent for a long while, staring out at the bay.

"What happened to Simon and Angelica?" Jan asked softly.

"Angelica died in the fire," Simon told her. "She is buried in the Fear Street cemetery in an unmarked grave. And Simon?" He shrugged. "Never seen or heard from again."

67

The candles flickered, the small flames bending down, then standing back up. Cari suddenly felt cold all over.

"I'm going to run up to the hotel and get a sweatshirt," Jan said, jumping up. "Cari, can I bring you one too?"

"Yeah. Thanks," Cari said.

"Don't tell any more stories till I get back," Jan told Simon. Then she disappeared up the dark dune toward the hotel.

"Such a terrible story," Cari said to Simon, shaking her head. "That's not the story we usually hear."

"Yeah. I always heard that Simon Fear was a vampire or something," Eric blurted out.

Simon chuckled, his face completely hidden in the shadows, his white suit seeming to float. "I don't know," he said, sounding very amused. "That would make *me* a vampire too—wouldn't it?"

No one said anything for a while.

Cari sat with her arms wrapped around her knees, staring at the orange oval of light from the flickering candles, thinking about Simon's story, about the Fear girls, about finding them without their bones.

After a while Simon broke the silence. "It's getting cold," he said quietly. "Maybe we should—"

He was interrupted by a shrill scream of terror.

They all jumped to their feet.

A second scream tore through the night air.

"It's coming from the hotel!" Eric exclaimed.

"It . . . it sounds like Jan!" Cari said.

Chapter 9

"PLEASE—NO PARTY!"

The candles flickered out.

Cari took off up the dune, followed by Eric and Craig.

The screams had stopped. The only sounds now were the thud of their sneakers over the sandy ground and the low wash of the bay behind them.

Be okay, Jan, Cari thought as she ran. Be okay. Please be okay. The words repeated over and over in her mind, taking on the rhythm of her legs as she ran.

Be okay. *Please* be okay.

I'll never forget those screams, she realized.

They repeated again and again in her ears, each time bringing a new stab of terror.

Please be okay.

Now the three of them were running past the pool house, past the dark rectangle of the swimming pool, across the terrace toward the back of the darkened hotel. Cari glanced behind her. Simon was struggling up the dune, several hundred yards away.

Cari was only a few yards from the back entrance when she saw the dark figure run out of the hotel, heading right toward her.

She opened her mouth to scream but stopped herself when she realized the dark figure was Jan.

"Jan!" She ran up to her friend and threw her arms around Jan's shoulders. "Are you okay?"

"I . . . I saw her!" Jan stammered, seemingly dazed.

"What happened?" both Eric and Craig cried, breathing heavily.

"What's the disturbance here?" Martin called, suddenly appearing from out of the darkness, sounding more irritated than concerned.

"I saw her," Jan repeated.

Cari took a step back. She and the two boys had formed a protective circle around Jan.

"What happened?" Simon called, scurrying across the terrace, his suit jacket flapping behind him as he ran. Martin hurried over to him.

"I . . . I saw the ghost!" Jan declared.

Eric groaned. "I don't believe this," he muttered.

"It was really there. I saw her," Jan insisted, her voice high with excitement. She tugged at the sides of her hair with both hands.

"Those screams . . ." Simon said, holding a hand over his heart.

"I'm sorry," Jan said. "I couldn't help it."

"I think we should all go inside," Martin said

impatiently. He took Simon by the elbow and led him to the door.

Cari and the others followed. A minute later they were all gathered in the lobby. Jan, tense and seemingly disoriented, took a seat on one of the big leather couches. Simon, still trying to catch his breath, sat beside her.

"It was down that hall," Jan said, pointing to the corridor that stretched to the left of the front desk. "That's where I saw the ghost. She seemed to come right through the wall."

"Hey, I thought that was *apple juice* we were drinking!" Eric cracked, expecting a big laugh. But no one even chuckled. Everyone was too interested in Jan's story.

"What did she look like?" Martin asked.

His voice startled Cari. She hadn't realized he was standing right beside her.

Tugging at a strand of her hair, Jan stared at the wall straight ahead of her, as if trying to picture the ghost. "She was kind of old-fashioned looking," she said thoughtfully. "Dressed all in white. Maybe it was a nightgown. Her hair was in a long braid that fell down her back. She was young, kind of pretty, I guess."

Jan shifted uncomfortably on the couch, still staring straight ahead at the wall. "It's her eyes that I remember most," she said. "Her face was pale. White as chalk. White as . . . death. But she had these eyes. They were big and black. They looked like lumps of coal. Like snowman eyes."

She started to say more, but her voice caught in

her throat. "Try to calm down a bit," Simon said softly, gently patting the back of Jan's hand. "Martin, why don't you go make her a cup of hot tea?"

"Very well," Martin said. But he made no attempt to move.

"She just stared at me with those coal black eyes," Jan continued. "They were so cold, so . . . mean. I think she was trying to frighten me. Everything was suddenly ice-cold. The room. The air. She kept staring at me. Lumps of coal on that dead white face. I screamed, and she vanished back into the wall. Just disappeared. Then I guess I screamed again."

Jan sat silently, twisting the strand of hair, staring at the wall.

Eric and Craig exchanged glances. Cari wondered what they were thinking. And she wondered what *she* was thinking! Someone—or something—had terrified Jan. Could it *really* have been a ghost?

"Are you okay now?" Cari asked Jan.

Jan didn't seem to hear her. She was far away, lost in her thoughts.

"These old inns contain many mysteries," Simon said, staring over at Martin meaningfully.

"She'll be back," Jan whispered. "The ghost will be back. I can feel it."

Cari couldn't sleep.

She propped the soft, goose-down pillow behind her and lay staring up at the shadows playing across the ceiling of her room. Outside, the black sky was clear and starry, and a soft white full moon appeared over the bay.

She found herself thinking about Lauren for some reason, wondering what Lauren had done that day. Probably hung around the backyard. Complained about having nothing to do. Or maybe played with the little girl who had moved in down the block, across the street from the old Fear mansion.

Why on earth am I thinking about Lauren? Cari asked herself. She realized she must be homesick.

She forced Lauren out of her mind and decided to think about Eric.

Eric?

He was so cute. She didn't even mind the diamond stud in his ear, which at first she had thought was a silly affectation.

And he seemed to be thinking about her too. She could tell. The way he kept looking at her during the long dinner. The way he kept smiling at her. That cute smile that made the dimple appear in one cheek.

Lauren? Eric?

Her mind certainly was skipping around tonight!

I'm just trying to avoid thinking about Jan and the ghost, she told herself.

She shivered. A ghost. Jan actually saw a ghost. It's here. It could be in this room right now, ready to pop out of the wall and stare at me with coal lump eyes.

I'll never get to sleep, she thought.

She sat up and put her feet down on the floor. The moon seemed to be hanging right outside her window. Its silver light formed a large rectangle across the carpet.

She stood up and, stepping into the light, walked over to the closet and found her robe. I'm going down to the kitchen to get something to drink, she decided.

She pulled her door open and stepped into the narrow hallway. It smelled of carpet cleaner and disinfectant. Dim night lights along the floor molding provided the only light.

Tying the belt around her robe, Cari began walking quietly down the long hallway. Her rubber thongs made no sound on the carpet. The doors on both sides of the hall were closed as always.

She turned a corner and headed down another corridor, identical in its smell, in its darkness, in its silence.

So quiet. Like walking in a dream.

And then a sudden sound.

She stopped. And held her breath.

It was just the floor creaking. It *had* to be the floor creaking.

Another loud creak, followed by a rattle.

The rattle of a chain?

No. That's silly, she told herself.

The rattling sound grew louder, nearer. Then stopped.

Another creak. And then a groan.

So soft. Almost like a human groan.

Strange, soft music seemed to float down the hall. Violins. Playing the same note.

And then she heard the whisper.

"Cari."

The whispered sound of her name.

No. I'm imagining it. It's just a breeze. Just a draft. It isn't a whisper. It isn't my name.

No.

The violins continued their sustained note, so softly she could barely hear it.

"Carrrrrrrrrrri."

It was whispering to her.

An invisible voice—a girl's voice—so close—right behind her—was whispering. Calling her name.

"No!" she shouted, not even realizing she had made the sound.

And now she was running down the corridor, stumbling in the awkward thongs, bursting around a corner, and down another dark hallway, doors closed on both sides.

"Carrrrrrri."

"No!"

She turned another corner, not seeing, not thinking, not even realizing that the terror was pushing her forward.

She knew only that she had to get away from the whisper, the ghostly whisper calling her name.

"Carrrrrri."

She ran to the end of the corridor, the hard soles of the thongs slapping against the flat carpet. Past a door marked Fire Escap — the final *e* having somehow escaped.

And then stopped when she heard voices.

Loud voices. Human voices.

Gulping air, struggling to stop the heaving of her chest, she didn't recognize the corridor she was in at first. The voices were coming from a room without a number.

A thin crack of light bled under the closed doorway. Voices were shouting on the other side.

The ghostly whisper had stopped.

She moved close and listened at the door.

It was Simon. She recognized his voice immediately. He seemed to be arguing with someone, heatedly, passionately.

She must be outside Simon's room, she realized.

Yes. It made sense. It was the first room on the corridor. Beside it stood the wide staircase that led down to the main lobby and the hotel office.

"Listen to me," Simon was shouting inside the room. "Listen to me!"

"No, I won't!" a voice replied, just as loudly, just as angrily.

A woman's voice!

Cari's mouth dropped open in surprise.

"Please, Simon, I'm begging you!" she heard the woman cry. "Please—no party! No party! Please!"

PART TWO

THE INVITATION

Chapter 10

A NIGHT VISITOR

Cari stood frozen outside the door. She listened longer, but the voices faded away as if their owners had drifted into another room.

What were they arguing about? Who was the woman? Could it be the ghost?

Just then she heard someone inside the room moving toward the door. Quickly she turned and ran down the hall. Thinking about the woman, about the argument she had overheard, about the mysterious party, Cari wandered the halls until she found her room.

But she knew she couldn't go to bed. She had to tell someone about the whispers and about the voices. She had to tell Jan.

She walked past her own room and knocked twice on Jan's door, softly the first time, then harder. Jan opened the door after the second knock. She was still in her jeans and sweatshirt. It was obvious that she hadn't even tried to get to sleep.

"Cari, what's the matter?" Jan asked, pulling Cari into her room. All the lights were on. Books and journals were scattered over the unmade bed.

"The ghost," Cari blurted out. "I think I heard it. I mean, I think it called me."

Jan didn't look at all surprised. She cleared a space on the edge of the bed and made Cari start at the beginning and relate all that she had seen and heard.

"We have to leave this place," Cari said after telling Jan everything. "We have to get out of here. Go home!"

"No, we can't," Jan insisted. "It's too exciting. Come on." She pulled Cari off the bed and into the hall. "Let's look for traces of the ghost," Jan whispered, still pulling Cari by the hand.

Cari suddenly felt very frightened. And very tired.

She didn't want to be out in the dark creepy hall searching for the ghost. She had had enough mysterious excitement for one night.

She yawned. "It must be three in the morning, Jan. Let's try to get some sleep."

Cari grabbed the doorknob to her room, then quickly jerked her hand away. "Hey—it's sticky!"

"Let me see that," Jan whispered and bent down to investigate the knob in the dim hall light. She put her fingers on the knob, then examined them. "I thought so," she said, a pleased smile forming on her face.

"What is it?" Cari asked.

"It's sticky, all right. Some sort of protoplasmic

substance. Ghosts have been known to leave this stuff behind after materializing."

"You mean like in *Ghostbusters?*" Cari asked.

"Yes," Jan replied, bringing her shadowy face close to Cari's. "But this *ain't no movie.*"

It was a beautiful, cool morning. Golden sunshine filled the room through the tall dining-room windows that overlooked the bay. Beyond the windows, the sky was solid blue, as if the color had been painted on in a single stroke.

At breakfast, buttering their fresh blueberry muffins, Cari and Jan told the boys about their adventures of the night before.

"So now *you* believe in this stuff too?" Eric asked Cari, making a face.

"I know what I heard," Cari said vehemently. "I'm not making anything up."

"The woman you heard could have been the cook," Craig suggested.

"No, it couldn't," Cari replied. "Remember? Simon told us the cook wouldn't be back until Friday."

"That's why Martin made our picnic dinner," Jan added. "The woman you heard in Simon's room *has* to be a ghost too. Maybe she and Simon are lovers. Maybe they've been lovers for a hundred years. Maybe Simon is really a vampire and the woman—"

Before she could develop her tale more, Martin appeared, glum as usual, carrying a red metal toolbox. "Ready to begin work?" he asked, frowning at them disapprovingly and gesturing across the dining room.

81

"Martin, is there a woman staying in this hotel?" Jan asked.

The question seemed to startle Martin. He appeared to flinch, as if he'd been physically stung by it. But he recovered quickly and his usual sour expression immediately returned. "No," he said blankly. "No woman."

"Did Simon have a visitor? A woman visitor?"

Martin gave her a sour look. "There's been no woman in Simon's room. Not since Greta died. Greta was his wife."

Then he turned and carried the toolbox to the back of the room. Jan looked over at Cari, puzzled. But the subject was dropped. It was time to get to work.

"This is where I'd like you to begin," Martin said, removing a huge oil painting of a lighthouse that had covered most of the wall. "Sand the molding first. Then you can remove the wallpaper in this area."

They worked all morning, removing the old brown paint from the molding. The room became hot and thick with brown dust from their efforts. It was hard work. There were several coats of paint on the old moldings, all of which were damp clear through to the wood from the wet sea air and difficult to remove.

"Break time!" Jan declared at about eleven-thirty. "Let's get something to drink. Then I want to try my aunt again. I get no answer every time I call. My parents haven't heard from her either!"

Eric leaped off the middle rung of his ladder and followed Jan and Craig across the room toward the kitchen. "I just want to finish this one spot," Cari called after them.

They didn't seem to hear her. She listened to their voices as they disappeared into the adjoining kitchen, then turned around on her ladder and went back to work. She was sanding a delicate corner molding, using a square sheet of sandpaper wrapped around a block of wood. Her arm muscles ached from having to hold her hand above her head.

She coughed and closed her eyes for a moment. If only there were some way to get the tiny paint flecks to fall *away* from her instead of *onto* her!

My hair must be filled with paint dust, she thought, sighing. Oh, well. It's almost lunchtime. And when we finish working, we can jump into the pool or hit the beach. Not a bad life.

That thought made her begin work again with renewed vigor. At least ten or fifteen minutes had gone by—she had lost exact track of the time— when she heard footsteps approaching.

"Eric? Is that you?"

She glanced across the room, somewhat off balance, into the face of a stranger.

He was a stranger and yet he wasn't. He had Simon's white hair and Simon's white mustache. He had Simon's ruddy complexion. But there the resemblance ended.

Where Simon was tall, and neat, and elegant, this man was hunched over, and very unkempt, his hair tousled and standing up in the back, with one flap of his gray sport shirt untucked from his baggy chino slacks, which were stained at the knee.

He wore a black eye patch over his right eye, and his face seemed frozen in a scowl. Over the wrinkled gray sport shirt, he had a loose-fitting safari jacket with several pockets, all of which seemed to be filled with pieces of folded-up paper, pens, and handkerchiefs. He carried a hunting rifle in his right hand, holding it by the barrel and using it as a cane. The stock tapped against the hard floor as he approached Cari.

"Hi," Cari said, smiling down at him from her perch on the ladder.

He grunted in reply, staring up at her with one clear, black eye, his scowling expression unchanging.

"I'm Cari Taylor." She waited for him to introduce himself, but he just stared at her. So she said, "You must be Edward."

"Edward Fear in the flesh," he said, turning the rifle over and leaning on the stock. His voice wasn't smooth and deep like his brother's. It was gruff, as gruff as he appeared to be.

How can two brothers be so different? Cari thought, staring down uncomfortably at him as he studied her, scratching his chest through his shirt with his free hand.

"My friends and I . . . we're working here. I mean, we're s-staying here," Cari stammered, feeling more and more ill at ease. If only his expression would change. If only he'd stop staring up at her with such cold intensity.

"I heard," he said impatiently. Using the rifle as a cane once again, he walked over to the windows and stood staring out. The bright sunlight brought out the drabness of his clothes. Cari could see that they were wrinkled and obviously dirty.

She remembered Simon saying that his brother was depressed. She guessed he was too depressed to care about his appearance.

What is he depressed *about?* she found herself wondering.

"It's a beautiful day," she said. "It's so pretty here." She couldn't decide whether to come down from the ladder and join him or continue working.

"It's too hot," he said sharply, correcting her. He continued to stare out at the ocean, slowly twirling the upturned barrel of the hunting rifle.

"It is very hot in here," Cari said.

Edward said nothing more, and Cari could feel her face reddening. Was he deliberately trying to make her feel uncomfortable?

Why didn't the others return? Where were they anyway?

"Where are the others?" Edward asked as if invading her thoughts.

"They . . . uh . . . took a break," Cari stammered. "Went to get something to drink. I'm just finishing up this corner here."

She pointed to it, but he didn't look up. "Quiet around here," he said with some sadness.

"It sure is," Cari said. "This place is so enormous. It feels funny with only five or six people in it."

He seemed displeased by her remark. He made an unpleasant face and, tapping the rifle noisily against the floor, stepped up to the foot of her ladder.

Suddenly frightened, Cari held her breath. She had the feeling he was going to climb up after her. Or grab her legs.

But he stopped a foot away and stared up at the molding.

Chill out, Cari told herself. You're losing it, kid. Edward is a little weird, but that's no reason to start imagining such crazy things.

He removed a handkerchief from one of the bulging pockets in his safari jacket and blew his nose loudly. Then he wiped his mustache, balled up the handkerchief, and shoved it into another pocket.

"Do a good job," he said, turning back to her.

"Yes. Uh . . . we will," Cari said, not sure how to reply to that remark.

"You see my brother?" he asked, his eyes taking in the empty dining room.

"No. Not this morning. He wasn't at breakfast," Cari said.

"I must see him," Edward said thoughtfully. His mind seemed to drift away to other matters.

"I'll tell him you're looking for him if he comes in here," Cari said.

"Do a good job," he repeated. And then, before she could reply, he quickly added, "I hope you and your friends will be here for the party."

The party?

Cari felt a sudden feeling of dread in the pit of her stomach. Edward's words made her remember the woman she had heard in Simon's room, the woman pleading, "Please—no party." The woman had sounded so desperate, so frightened.

"Please—no party!"

"What party?" Cari asked Edward.

"I *insist* you stay for the party. Make no plans to leave," he said, and walked from the room.

Am I doing the right thing? Cari asked herself.

When Eric asked her to go for a late-night walk on the beach, she hesitated. They had been friends for so long, she wasn't sure she wanted anything more to develop.

A summer romance.

That wasn't the idea of coming to Piney Island. All four of them had agreed. Well, they hadn't actually said it out loud. It was just sort of understood.

They were coming to meet *new* kids.

But there *are* no new kids, Cari thought. And Eric looks so cute. His face is already tanned. His long hair smells so clean, like the sea air. He looks like a real beach bum, she thought, in his sleeveless blue T-shirt, faded denim cutoffs, and sandals.

"Where are Jan and Craig?" she asked, trying to decide whether or not to go with him. She wanted to go, but she was just trying to figure out if there were any major compelling reasons not to.

"They're both completely wrecked," he said, smiling. "They went to their rooms."

"Everyone seemed really exhausted at dinner," Cari said. "Simon too. He barely said three words."

"And where was his brother Edward?" Eric asked. "So far, Cari, you're the only one who's seen him. Weird!"

"I know," Cari said. "Jan, of course, thinks Edward is a ghost."

"Jan thinks *I'm* a ghost!" Eric cracked.

"Well, she has an excuse for acting weird—she's really worried about her aunt," Cari said. "Jan tried calling at Aileen's all day. But the phone just rings and rings. Nobody answers. Rose should have been here by now. Where is she? And why doesn't she call?"

"Weird," Eric repeated. "So, how about this walk? You and me. What do you say?"

He was so cute. How could she resist?

Besides, what was wrong with a nice walk before bedtime on a beautiful, moonlit beach?

And the beach truly was beautiful. Holding Eric's hand, she stared out at the reflection of the full moon rippling in the rolling, dark bay waters. "It's so bright," she said. "Everything is so clear."

"Yeah. I like the way wet sand feels on my toes," Eric said. "You know—that cold, soggy feeling."

"You're very poetic tonight," Cari cracked.

They had stopped at the water's edge, but he hadn't let go of her hand.

Cari turned to look up at the hotel. A soft wind was blowing the tall weeds that climbed the sloping dune. The weeds seemed to bend in waves. Everything seemed so soft, so liquid. The quiet waves, the shadowy sand, the bending weeds.

It was as if the pale moonlight had softened everything, even the darkness.

Eric kissed her, catching her by surprise.

His lips felt hard against hers.

No, she thought.

This wasn't the idea.

This wasn't what was supposed to happen.

Yes, she thought.

Yes, it's okay.

She kissed him back.

He had his hands on her bare shoulders. His hands felt so warm, so safe.

The kiss lasted a long, long time.

A shuffling noise from the rocks near the dock made her pull away.

"What was that?"

Was someone watching them?

"I think it was just water hitting the rock," Eric said, his face still close to hers.

She could still taste his lips on hers. Salty.

"Let's go back inside," she said, suddenly chilled.

"Sure."

He took her hand and they made their way up to the hotel. Cari stopped halfway up the dune to check out the rocks. No one there.

The only sound now was the steady splash of the low waves against the shore and the whisper of the wind blowing through the beach grass. So why did she have the frightening feeling that she and Eric weren't alone?

Ghosts, she thought.

They're everywhere.

Still holding Eric's hand, she ran the rest of the way, not looking back once. She didn't feel safe until she was back in her room with the door securely locked.

Chapter 11

A DARK SECRET

"Let's get to work," Eric said, standing up from the dining-room table and stretching. He studied the sky beyond the windows. "At least it won't be too hot today with the sun behind those clouds."

Cari took a last bite of blueberry muffin, then followed them to the back of the room. She bent down to open the tool chest on the floor beside the scaffolding Martin and Eric had rigged up. "Come on, guys," she said. "Who's going to get up there first?" She raised her eyes to their unfinished work. They had managed to remove the paint from one ten-foot section of ceiling molding. But there were still two large sections to be done on that one side.

"There's only room for two on the scaffold," Eric said. "Why don't Craig and I start, and then you and Jan can take over when our arms get tired. Or one of you can use the ladder."

Cari nodded her agreement. She helped Eric lift

the heavy electrical sander up to the scaffold floor. Their hands touched. He gazed into her eyes. She thought for a brief second that he was going to kiss her. She knew they were both thinking of their walk along the beach the past night. Thinking of their kiss.

Eric's face reddened and he backed away, turning to Craig. "Okay, man, let's get to work." He climbed up onto the scaffold and helped Craig up after him.

"This thing is kinda wobbly," Craig said, glancing down at Cari.

"No, it isn't. *You're* kinda wobbly!" Eric said. He hoisted up the sander and began to raise it to the molding. "Hey, it's broken."

"It isn't plugged in," Craig said, staring at the plug, which was lying beside the outlet on the floor.

"Hi, guys." Jan came up behind Cari, a worried look on her face.

"Did you reach your aunt?"

"No. No answer," Jan told her, making a face. "It rang and rang, but no one picked up. I just don't understand it."

"Is Simon going to Provincetown to see what the story is?"

Jan shrugged. "I don't know. I searched for him when I got off the phone, but couldn't find him." She said something else, but Cari couldn't hear it. Eric had started up the sander, and its deafening whine as it whirred against the molding drowned out Jan's words.

Both Jan and Cari took a step back. Paint dust filled the air. Cari reached into the tool chest for two protective masks. She started to hold one out to Jan when Craig screamed.

"Whoa! Look out!"

Startled, she raised her head in time to see the scaffold sway, first to the right, then to the left.

Then, as both boys screamed, it collapsed with a loud cracking sound.

It all happened so fast, Cari wasn't sure it was really falling. Eric, his mouth open in shock, held tightly onto the loud, whirring sander. Craig, screaming at the top of his lungs, grabbed at the wall as if trying to hold himself up.

The scaffolding and the two boys hit the floor with a loud crash.

Eric toppled onto his back, the sander leaping from his hand. It bounced once, then stopped at Cari's feet.

Craig somehow managed to stay on his feet. "Oh, wow!" He was obviously stunned though. He had pulled off a section of the flowered wallpaper as he fell.

"Are you okay?" Cari and Jan both screamed.

The boys slowly nodded. "Yeah. Fine, I guess," Eric said, getting to his feet, testing his right shoulder.

"Yeah. I'm okay too. But look at this," Craig said, the wallpaper still gripped tightly in his hand.

Where the wallpaper had been stood a wooden door.

"Somebody wallpapered right over a door!" Craig exclaimed, finally dropping the wallpaper.

"I guess that big picture covered it up. Weird,"

Eric muttered, still working his shoulder muscles. He moved up to the door and pulled away more of the wallpaper.

"Why would anyone do that?" Cari asked, stepping closer.

"Get away from it," Jan said, surprising everyone with the urgency of her words. "It had to be covered for a reason. A good reason."

"Give us a break, Jan," Eric said, rolling his eyes.

"Don't touch the door. I'm warning you," Jan said, very pale and frightened. "It's evil. I can feel it."

Eric laughed. Craig laughed too, but uncertainly. He took a step back.

Cari put a hand on Jan's shoulder. "If Jan feels so strongly about it, maybe we should just forget about the door," she told the boys.

"Yeah, maybe," Craig agreed.

But Eric ignored them all. He began tearing away the remaining wallpaper. In a few seconds the entire door was exposed. The wood was smooth and shiny, almost new looking, probably because it hadn't been exposed to the air.

"Let's see what's behind Door Number One!" Eric exclaimed.

There was no doorknob. Just a small hole where a knob had once been attached. Turning to grin back at Cari, Eric reached his fingers into the hole and pulled.

"No—don't!" Jan warned.

Eric ignored her.

The door pulled open easily.

"Eric—please!" Jan wailed.

"There's some kind of passageway back there," Eric said, poking his head into the open doorway.

"Huh? Passageway?"

The other three stepped forward to peer into the dark tunnel.

And with a hideous ear-shattering screech, something leaped out of the darkness at them.

Chapter 12

TRAPPED

"*H*elp! It's a bat!"

All four of them screamed and dodged away. Cari heard the flapping of its wings and felt a cold *whoosh* of air against her cheek before she saw it swoop out of the doorway, narrowly missing her.

She screamed again and hit the floor.

"It's okay. It flew out the window," Craig shouted, sounding very relieved.

All four of them regrouped at the doorway, breathing hard.

"I hate bats!" Cari declared. "Bats and spiders." She shuddered.

"There may be more bats in there," Jan said, her skin very pale. "Let's just close the door and pretend it doesn't exist."

"Oh, come on, Jan," Cari said impatiently. "This is kind of nifty, don't you think? A hidden door. A secret passageway. This is your kind of thing, isn't it?"

Jan didn't reply. She just stared into the darkness beyond the open door.

"This isn't like you," Cari continued. "You should be the one urging *us* on to explore the hidden passageway."

Smiling, Eric gestured with both hands, as if to say, "After you."

"I just have a bad feeling about this," Jan said, shaking her head. "A premonition. Don't you ever have premonitions?" She gripped the ivory skull on the chain around her neck and squeezed it hard.

"Sometimes," Cari said. "But, come on. This could be fun. Maybe we'll find where the ghost lives, Jan."

"Maybe you'll find a room full of ghosts, my child," Eric said, doing a terrible Count Dracula impersonation.

"And ghouls," Craig added. "Don't forget the ghouls."

"Come on, boys and ghouls. Let's check it out," Cari urged. "How often do you find secret hallways hidden behind the wallpaper?"

"This is the first one I've found in *days!*" Eric joked.

Cari pushed past him and peered into the passageway. It was a low, narrow tunnel. The walls appeared to be made of plaster—the floor concrete. Dim yellow light came from somewhere at the far end, around a corner, maybe. "There are two flashlights in the tool chest," Cari told Eric. "I think we're going to need them."

Craig pulled the flashlights from the chest and handed one to Cari. "What if Simon comes in?" he asked.

"We'll tell him we took a break to go exploring," Cari said. "I wonder if he knows about this secret passageway. I wonder if Martin knows. He's the one who told us to start in this corner, remember." She turned to Jan, who had stepped cautiously through the doorway and was standing right behind her. "You okay?"

"Yeah. Fine," Jan said dryly.

"You still have a premonition?" Cari asked.

"Yeah. But I'm starting to get into this," Jan said. "This *is* my kind of thing, after all." She forced a smile to her face.

The two flashlights threw down bright cones of light as they began to walk down the dark, empty tunnel. The concrete floor felt hard under their sneakers. It was cool and very damp. Cari reached out and felt the wall. It was wet.

"What's *that?*" Eric cried.

Something walked into the wavering spotlight of Craig's flashlight.

"Yuck!" Cari cried. "That's the biggest bug I've ever seen. What *is* it?"

"It's as big as a tarantula," Craig said, almost in awe.

"Squish it," Eric said, his voice a whisper.

"You squish it!" Craig replied. He kept his light on it. The enormous beetlelike bug disappeared around a corner.

"It wasn't a spider—*was* it?" Cari asked in a tiny, frightened voice.

97

"It was some other kind of giant bug," Eric said, not very reassuringly.

"I . . . I want to go back," Cari said, suddenly overcome with fear.

"Huh?" Eric cried, taking her flashlight from her. "Come on, Cari. We just started." He took her hand and led her forward.

After a while the tunnel curved to the right, and then sloped down. They walked slowly, cautiously, keeping the two cones of light steady in front of them. After a few minutes they came to a fork. Two passageways led from the first in different directions.

"We're going down," Eric said. "I'll bet one of these tunnels leads down through the dunes to the water."

"Wonder why it was built," Craig said, keeping close to Eric as they followed the passageway to the right.

"Probably for escape," Eric said.

"Escape from *what?*" Cari asked.

"Actually, there used to be a lot of smuggling in this area," Jan told them. "This tunnel may be an old smugglers' tunnel. The smugglers could sneak their cargo right from the beach into the inn without being seen. They designed them like mazes with lots of twists and turns in case they were followed."

They followed the curve of the tunnel, which branched off into two other tunnels. "Which way, Captain Kidd?" Craig asked Jan.

"Let's take the one on the right," Jan said.

They turned right and walked a few hundred yards more.

Suddenly Cari uttered a soft cry.

"Cari, what's wrong?" Jan asked. All four of them had stopped.

"Those . . . webs!" Cari pointed up.

They pointed the two flashlights to the ceiling where giant cobwebs were strung so thick the light couldn't penetrate them.

Cari gasped aloud, then felt her breath catch in her throat.

"Where there are cobwebs there are bound to be spiders," Eric said, shining the flashlight up at the webs.

"And if there are spiders," Jan added, "there has to be a way for them to get in here. I'll bet I'm right. I'll bet this tunnel leads to the beach."

Sure enough, enormous, pale spiders, the size of grapes, hovered just above their heads. The spiders swayed to and fro, as if blown by an invisible air current. As they swayed, their slender legs curled and uncurled in the light of the flashlights, as if beckoning to the four intruders.

With Jan in the lead, the four friends began to run past them. They continued to follow the twisting tunnel until they came to a wooden doorway, set into the plaster wall.

It was open a few inches, pitch black inside.

"Anybody home?"

Jan knocked on the door.

The sound of the knock echoed eerily down the empty passageway.

"Anybody in there?" Jan called again.

"What are you waiting for?" Cari asked impatiently. She stepped in front of Jan and impulsively pushed the door open.

It creaked noisily, as if in protest.

Cari peered into the room behind the doorway. "I don't believe this!"

It was a small room, just big enough for the four of them to squeeze in, bare except for a small wooden table with benches in the center. The walls were dark, red in the light of the flashlights, as if blood had dripped down them.

"Oh!" Eric cried as the light from his flashlight fell on an object on top of the table.

It was a skull, a human skull.

"Let's get out of here," Craig said, sounding genuinely scared.

Jan bravely reached out and lifted the skull off the table. "It's real," she said.

"Hope it isn't someone we know," Eric cracked.

Jan replaced the skull. "Hey—my fingers. Look." She held out her hand for the others to see. Eric shone his light onto it.

"What's that sticky stuff?" he asked.

"It's protoplasm. Left by a ghost," Jan said, and she couldn't keep a triumphant smile from crossing her face.

"You mean—?" For the first time, Eric had lost his skepticism.

"Maybe now you'll all believe me," Jan said, examining her sticky fingers. "This is a well-known supernatural phenomenon. A ghost has materialized in this room. Recently."

The skull suddenly rolled backward on the table-top, the sunken eyes staring up at them.

"I'm outta here!" Eric yelled.

The other three were already heading for the door.

Once out in the dark tunnel, they didn't stop. They began running, the light from their flashlights darting wildly over the walls and floor.

They didn't stop running until they reached the door leading to the dining room. Breathing hard, Cari eagerly reached for the door and pushed.

It didn't move.

"Hey!"

She pushed again—harder.

Again the door didn't budge.

"It's stuck or something," she told the others.

"Let me try," Eric said.

Cari stepped back. Eric had no more success than she had had.

"Weird," he said, concerned.

He tried again. Then Craig moved beside him and they both pushed against the door.

"It's been jammed shut or something," Eric said, looking very alarmed in the harsh yellow light from the flashlight. "We're trapped in here."

Chapter 13

LOST FOREVER

"*L*et us out!" Cari screamed. She began pounding on the solid wood door with both fists. "Somebody—can you hear me? Let us out!"

Eric moved quickly to help, pounding on the door with his fists.

"Let us out! Let us out!" all four of them chanted.

They stopped to listen.

Silence greeted them from the other side of the door.

No one was out there.

"Did someone lock us in?" Jan asked suddenly, her voice unsteady, frightened.

Eric turned away from the door. "There's got to be another way out of here," he said. "Let's go back and follow the tunnel till we find it."

"No," Cari said, her fear speaking for her.

"Cari, we don't really have a choice," Eric said softly. "We can't get out this door. There's got to be another way out. Let's go find it."

Cari was outvoted three to one, so she reluctantly agreed. Huddling together, walking quickly behind the sweep of the flashlights, they turned away from the door and walked back through the narrow tunnel.

This time, when they reached the part where the tunnel divided in two, they took the passageway to the left.

"What was that?" Cari cried, feeling something scamper over her feet.

Or had she just imagined it?

Cari felt herself gripped with panic. She realized she was gasping for air. Her heart was pounding so hard in her chest, it hurt.

"Stop!" she cried.

Startled by the panic in her voice, the other three stopped. They drew close together. Craig and Eric kept the flashlights aimed at the ceiling so that light reflected down on them. In the dim light, Cari could see the same panic, the same fear, *her* panic, *her* fear, reflected on the shadowy faces of her friends.

"I'm sorry," she said. "I'll force myself to calm down. We'll find a way out of here. I know we will."

Eric put an arm around her shoulders. They walked quickly, the light darting at their feet.

Again, the passageway divided.

"Let's go this way," Jan said, heading right.

They turned into another tunnel, then into another that seemed to follow a wide curve. Water dripped from the ceiling. *Ping ping ping* against the concrete floor.

They made another choice, this time to the left, then turned into a passageway filled with spiders and spiderwebs.

"It doesn't seem to be leading us anywhere," Cari said dispiritedly.

"There should be an opening or a doorway or something," Craig said, his voice a frightened whisper.

"I think we've been here already," Jan said, her dark eyes wide with fright. "I remember that weird crack in the wall. I think maybe we're walking in circles."

"We're lost," Eric said glumly, lowering his flashlight in despair.

"Lost forever," Craig muttered to himself.

"Maybe this whole thing is a trap," Jan said.

"That's it, Jan. Look on the bright side," Eric cracked bitterly.

"Maybe it isn't a trap," Jan said. "But it's as good as a trap. These tunnels all look alike, and just keep winding forever. We'll *never* find our way out."

Chapter 14

THE VISITOR

"We have no choice. We have to keep walking till we find a way out," Cari said, wrapping her arms around herself, trying to warm herself from the cool dampness of the passageway. "We'll find it eventually."

Who blocked the dining-room door? Who locked us in? she wondered. Who could it have been?

There's no time to think about that now, she scolded herself.

They turned a corner and entered another long branch of the tunnel that sloped sharply up.

Have we been here before? Cari wondered.

She couldn't tell.

She could feel her panic start to rise, choking her. Her heart was thudding in her chest. She was suddenly aware of every breath she took and had the feeling that if she didn't concentrate on every breath, she would stop breathing.

"It must be lunchtime," Craig said in the shadowy, shifting light from his flashlight. "Martin will be looking for us."

"Maybe he could deliver our lunch to us here," Eric said.

"You're not funny," Cari muttered.

"Just trying to keep it light," Eric said.

As he said this, the tunnel suddenly brightened. Two narrow slits of daylight appeared in front of them.

"Yaay!" Eric cried. All four of them began running toward the bright light.

Cari quickly saw that it was a small hatch doorway. She was the first one to push the door open and scramble out of the tunnel. Blinking in the intense daylight, she had to cup a hand over her eyes to look around.

"We're on the beach!" Jan cried happily. "I was right!"

The tunnel opening was dug into one of the steep dunes along the bay beach. The opening faced away, at an angle that couldn't be seen by sunbathers on the beach.

"Doesn't the fresh air smell great!" Cari exclaimed.

"I was never so happy to see real sunlight," Craig said, stretching luxuriously, turning his face up to the sun.

"We can't stand out here sunbathing," Eric said. "We'd better get back to the hotel."

Laughing and joking, they made their way up the beach, crossed the terrace beside the deserted swimming pool, and reentered through the sliding glass dining-room doors.

The laughing stopped when they stepped into the dining room and up to the tunnel entrance.

"The scaffold . . . look!" Craig said.

They didn't need to have it pointed out to them. The others were all staring at it already.

The scaffolding, they saw immediately, had been moved. It had been pushed in front of the doorway.

This was why the door wouldn't open.

Someone had deliberately trapped them inside the tunnel.

The four of them spent the afternoon at the beach trying to relax, but they were unable to put the tunnel and the fact that someone had deliberately blocked their exit out of their minds.

Who had it been? Edward? Martin?

"We've got to tell Simon everything at dinner tonight," Cari said. They all agreed.

Unfortunately, Simon did not appear at dinner. As Cari set her chowder bowl to one side and passed the tray of crabmeat salad to Eric, seated at the dining-room table beside her, Edward limped noisily into the room.

He was leaning on his hunting rifle, as before, using it as a cane. His face was red, angry red, ringed by his long white hair, which was unruly and unbrushed. He was wearing the same safari jacket Cari had seen him in during their first encounter. It was open, revealing a pale yellow sport shirt underneath with two buttons missing.

"Uh . . . Edward, I don't think you've met my friends," Cari said awkwardly, feeling her face redden.

Edward stared at her as if he didn't know her either. Cari introduced Jan, Eric, and Craig.

He scowled at them in greeting and muttered something that Cari couldn't hear. Then, setting the rifle down on the floor beside him, he took Simon's usual seat at the head of the table and began to slurp up his bowl of clam chowder noisily, rapidly, without glancing up once.

All conversation stopped. Everyone just stared at Edward, who finished his chowder in less than a minute and, still scowling angrily, pulled his salad plate closer and began gobbling up chunks of salad.

"Is . . . is Simon coming to dinner?" Cari finally managed to ask, breaking the uncomfortable silence.

Edward chewed for a while, staring at her the whole time. "No," he said finally. "Simon isn't here." He shoved another forkful of salad into his mouth.

"He left the hotel?" Cari asked.

Edward nodded and chewed noisily.

How can he be such a slob, Cari thought, while his brother is so neat, so elegant?

Edward seemed to be the opposite of Simon in every way. Simon was so outgoing, so jolly, so friendly and warm. Edward seemed cold, angry . . . depressed.

"Simon went to the mainland," Edward said in his gruff voice. "Provincetown." He grunted something else that Cari couldn't hear.

"To check on my aunt?" Jan asked eagerly.

Edward squinted his one good eye at her, as if seeing her for the first time. "Yeah. Your aunt."

He returned to his dinner. After he finished his salad, Martin served him a plate of roast chicken and mashed potatoes, a different dinner from everyone else's. Edward finished the meal in silence, as did everyone else.

It's as if he's brought a chill to the room, Cari thought. He's not making the tiniest attempt to be friendly or pleasant. He's just totally ignoring us.

She breathed a sigh of relief when he abruptly stood up, picked up his hunting rifle, and stalked out without a word. The whole room seemed to brighten, and Cari found herself laughing for no reason at all, just relief.

"He's a load of laughs," Eric said.

"Simon said he was depressed," Jan said thoughtfully.

"Well, he sure depressed *me!*" Cari cracked.

All four of them started to talk about Edward at once. Craig did a pretty good impression of Edward rapidly slurping his chowder.

They were still laughing when Martin appeared from the kitchen, appearing even more unpleasant than usual.

"You've got to listen to me!" Martin cried in a loud whisper. "There's not much time. *Please*— you must get out!"

"Huh? Get out of the dining room?" Eric blurted out.

All four of them were confused by Martin's statement.

"You don't understand," Martin said, still whispering. He started to say something else, but stopped. His eyes grew wide as he stared at the doorway.

Cari turned to see Edward leaning on his rifle, moving quickly back into the dining room. "Making a speech, Martin?" Edward said, more of a growl than a question.

Martin seemed to shrivel up. He hunched his shoulders. His face seemed to disappear into his jacket. "No, sir."

Edward stared at Martin for what seemed an eternity before Martin cast his eyes down to the floor.

Finally Edward broke the tense silence. "Perhaps you should return to your kitchen duties and stop disturbing Simon's guests," he said coldly. He shifted his weight, leaning down hard against the stock of the hunting rifle.

"Yes, sir."

Martin turned quickly and scurried off to the kitchen like a frightened mouse.

A pleased smile crossed Edward's face, but only briefly. It was the first time Cari had seen him smile.

He really enjoyed frightening Martin, Cari thought.

And why is Martin so scared of Edward?

It seemed to Cari that Martin was as hard and cold as Edward. He didn't seem to be the type to play the humble servant and cower like a wimp at his master's stern glance.

But Martin had definitely cowered—and he had scampered away very frightened.

I wish Simon was here, Cari thought, checking

out Eric beside her. He seemed to be thinking the same thing.

Edward's satisfied smile lasted only a brief second. Then his face fell back into its hard scowl, and without a word to the four teenagers, he headed out of the dining room, the hunting rifle tapping loudly.

"This is boring," Cari groaned. They'd been playing Scrabble in the rec room for over an hour.

"What kind of a word is *dis?*" Jan demanded.

"You know," Eric said. "I *dissed* you. Edward really *dissed* Martin tonight." He laughed.

"Give me a break." Jan tossed a handful of letters at Eric, who toppled off the hassock he'd been sitting on.

All four of them were tossing letter squares at one another when a tall figure appeared in the doorway.

"What a remarkable Scrabble game," Simon said, chuckling.

He stepped into the center of the room. He was dressed in white, as usual, a white, long-sleeved pullover and white linen trousers.

Cari and the others stopped their free-for-all.

"I've been to Provincetown," Simon told Jan.

"Yes. Edward told us," Jan said, her face filling with concern. "Aunt Rose . . . is she—?"

"She's fine," Simon said, smiling reassuringly. "I'm terribly sorry. It seems she did call. She spoke to Edward. When he told her what our situation was, Aileen convinced her to go to some kind of spa for a couple of days. I apologize for Edward. My poor brother forgets things these days."

"So she's feeling okay?" Jan asked.

"Yes, yes. As fit as a fiddle," Simon said. And then he added, "I guess that expression really dates me." He made a face. "Anyway, Rose will be here in a couple of days. She's taking the launch from Provincetown on Thursday."

"Great," Jan said, obviously very relieved. "It was so nice of you to go to all that trouble."

"No trouble," Simon said, raising a hand in protest. "No trouble at all, my dear. I was worried about Rose too. But now there is nothing to worry about."

Yes, there *are* still things to worry about, Cari thought. There's Martin. And Edward. And that secret tunnel with the weird room. And the ghost— Plenty of things to worry about.

"Simon—" Cari started. She had to ask him. She had to tell him the things they had seen.

"Simon—"

But he had vanished from the room.

Go away, world. Go away.

Jan, her eyes shut tight, her face clenched in a grimace of concentration, sat in her silky green pajamas on the area rug at the foot of her bed. Chanting softly to herself, she leaned forward, her fingertips tracing the circle and star she had chalked on the floor.

The room smelled of mothballs. She had opened the window wide to let in the fresh fragrant air. But now the chirping of crickets and tree frogs, a deafening symphony, was invading her thoughts, spoiling her concentration.

Go away, world. Go away.

Rolling her fingertips over the ancient symbol, she let herself drift, allowed herself to float, away from the chirping insects, the rush of the night wind, away from the damp, musty smells of the old hotel room.

She was floating through darkness now, soft and silent.

And still she continued to trace the chalked pentacle, feeling her fingers grow warm, feeling the floor come alive beneath her fingers.

Floating through the silent darkness.

All alone.

Alone and away.

And then suddenly she knew she wasn't alone.

She could feel the ghostly presence. She knew it was nearby. She knew it was floating to her.

I am drawn to the supernatural because I can sense it all around me. I have spirit powers, she thought, rubbing the pentacle, her hand throbbing with pain, with fire, with *life*.

Come to me, she thought. Come to me.

I can sense your presence. I know you're there, spirit.

"Reveal yourself!" she cried aloud.

The loud knock on the door startled her to her feet, eyes open, heart thudding.

Not with fear. But with anticipation.

I know you're there. I can feel it. I can sense it.

Her hand throbbed. With power.

The power coursed through her body, filled her with energy from the spirits all around.

Without hesitating, she pulled open the door.

"Oh!" she cried.

Chapter 15

THE FIRST SHOT

Jan wasn't at breakfast the next morning, but that wasn't unusual. She liked to sleep in, skip breakfast, and join them after the work had started.

"Good news about Jan's aunt," Craig said, helping himself to another plate of scrambled eggs and bacon. "Jan really was relieved."

"Yeah," Cari agreed uneasily.

Eric smiled at her, then moved his eyes past her to the big dining-room windows. "Not a beach day today," he said, smoothing the front of his Grateful Dead T-shirt with an open hand.

Cari saw that the sky was gray with heavy clouds that pressed all the way to the ground. A steady drizzle came down, the wind bending the grasses on the dune as if a giant foot were stepping on them.

"Yuck," she said, turning back to her cereal bowl.

"Well, we'll get a lot of work done," Eric said

cheerily. "We can probably get all the paper stripped on that side, and finish up the molding too."

"Anybody up for another tunnel adventure?" Craig asked brightly.

Eric and Cari both made disapproving faces and didn't bother to reply.

They worked the rest of the morning and didn't break for lunch until one-thirty.

"So where's Jan?" Cari asked as they washed their hands in the big steel sink in the kitchen. "She never sleeps *this* late."

"Yeah, you're right," Eric agreed, glancing around as if expecting to see her in the kitchen.

"She's probably off with Simon or Edward," Craig suggested. "We haven't seen either of them today."

"Yeah. Maybe she and Simon took the dinghy to Provincetown to see Rose," Eric said, drying his hands on the legs of his jeans.

"I think she would have told us if she was going somewhere," Cari said.

"Well, you're not worried about her, are you?" Eric asked, his face showing his concern. "We could form a search party."

"No, I'm not worried," Cari lied. "I'm sure you're right. She's probably off with Simon."

Martin, who also hadn't been seen since breakfast, had left cold sandwiches and drinks for them in the refrigerator.

They ate quickly in the gray light of the cavernous dining room. It was thundering outside. The dark sky had continued to rumble even though the steady rain of the morning had momentarily stopped.

They worked all afternoon, stripping wallpaper. The door to the hidden passageway was completely revealed but none of the three friends felt the slightest desire to open it or venture back into the twisting, dark tunnels.

At four-thirty they put down their tools, pushed the scaffolding against the wall, and went upstairs to take showers.

Passing Jan's room, Cari stopped, hesitated at the door, then knocked.

Silence.

She turned the knob and pushed the door open. All of the lights were on. Jan's bed was unmade. There were clothes tossed on the armchair and across the bed.

Nothing unusual.

But no sign of Jan.

"Where are you, Jan?" Cari called aloud.

The only reply was a creaking from the hallway, just the old hotel settling.

They heard Simon come in the front door as they ate dinner in the dining room, and watched as he passed the doors, walking quickly, not pausing to glance in.

"Simon?" Cari called. She wanted to ask if he knew where Jan was.

But he didn't seem to hear her. He went straight up the stairs to his room.

"Hey, you know what? I really *am* worried about Jan," Cari admitted to Eric and Craig.

As if on cue, Martin entered from the kitchen, carrying a tray. "Where is the dark-haired one?" he asked.

"You haven't seen her?" Cari asked.

Martin shook his head.

"We assumed she was with Simon," Craig said. "Did he go to Provincetown or something?"

Again Martin shook his head. "Simon went to see the workers, to find out when they planned to return. I haven't seen your friend."

Martin's words sent a stab of fear to Cari's chest. Her eyes followed him as he turned and went back to the kitchen.

"We've got to look for Jan," Cari said, suddenly cold all over. "Should we split up or stay together?"

"Stay together," Eric replied quickly. "We'll start upstairs."

"Where can she be?" Craig asked, shaking his head.

"Maybe the ghost got her," Cari said.

Eric gave her a searching look, then shook his head. "It wasn't a ghost who moved the scaffolding against the door," he said heatedly.

"Eric's right," Craig agreed quickly. "It had to be Martin—or Edward. Let's forget about ghosts."

"Let's just find Jan," Cari said.

They began their search in Jan's room. There were no clues, Cari realized. All of Jan's things seemed to be there. It was impossible to tell if she had slept in the bed or not.

A chalked pentacle had been half-rubbed into the floor at the foot of the bed. Cari saw it first and pointed it out to the boys. "If she summoned the ghost and the ghost took her somewhere . . ." Cari started.

Craig and Eric were determined not to talk about ghosts.

Are they afraid there just might *be* a ghost? Cari wondered, following them out of Jan's room, closing the door softly behind her.

They searched in all the rooms along the hallway of the old wing, without success. Then they searched the lobby and the adjoining rec room. They looked in the office, which was dark and silent.

Carrying flashlights, they ventured onto the terrace. The rain had stopped, but the sky was still blanketed with low clouds. The air was hot and wet, and Cari felt as if they were walking through a giant steam bath.

"Jan—where are you?" she called as they walked past the pool, the water nearly to the top because of all the rain.

No sign of her.

"This is scary," Cari said. She grabbed Eric's hand. Despite the steaminess of the night, it was ice-cold.

"We have to tell Simon she's missing," Eric said.

"We can call the Willow Island police," Cari said, not letting go of Eric's hand. Willow Island was larger, only ten minutes away by motorboat.

"Do you know where Simon's room is?" Craig asked as they headed back toward the hotel, walking quickly, their flashlights pointed at the wet sandy ground.

"I think I can find it," Cari said. And then she couldn't hold her fear back any longer. *"Where can Jan be? I'm so scared!"* she cried, sounding like a little girl. "This was supposed to be a fun summer. But instead we're in this creepy, empty place, with ghosts and horrible tunnels and skulls with sticky stuff all over them. I just want to get *out* of here."

Eric put an arm around her shoulders. "We'll find Jan," he said softly. "Simon will know where she is." His words were comforting, but his eyes reflected her fear.

"I hope Simon hasn't gone to bed," Craig said.

Even cool Craig is scared, Cari thought, glancing at his troubled face.

"It's still early," Cari said, checking her watch. "It isn't even eight-thirty." She stopped in front of the door at the top of the stairs, the door with no room number. "This is it."

She raised her hand to knock.

A loud cry made her pull her hand away.

At first she thought that Eric had cried out.

But she quickly realized that the cry had come from inside the room.

All three of them moved closer to the door to listen.

Another cry. A man's voice.

Someone was yelling.

A heated argument was taking place inside. Frightened, Cari pulled Eric and Craig back a few steps.

Simon was yelling at Edward. Edward's voice was gruff in reply.

And then the woman shouted out her disapproval of both of them.

Cari gripped Eric's hand tightly. "Did you hear her too?" she whispered.

"The woman?" Eric asked, his face close to her ear, his hand squeezing hers more tightly.

"You're crazy!" the woman screamed.

"Who are you calling crazy?" Edward replied, his voice filled with menace.

"You're *both* crazy," the woman insisted. "You should be locked up."

"I'm warning you—" Edward threatened.

"Leave her alone!" Simon cried, sounding frightened.

"Don't defend her. She doesn't need you to defend her," Edward snapped. "You're worthless. Worthless."

"You're not frightening us, Edward," the woman insisted.

"Hey!" Simon shouted suddenly. "Don't do that!"

Cari grabbed Eric's arm. Was the argument on the other side of the door turning into a real fight?

"I won't stay for the party," the woman was shouting inside the room.

"You don't have a choice," Edward shouted back at her, his voice rough, his tone ugly.

"You'd better listen to Edward," Cari heard Simon say. "I've begged him and begged him. But to no avail. Edward, if you'd only listen to reason—"

"You keep out of this!" Edward bellowed at the top of his lungs. "I've already warned you—"

"Edward, please—" the woman cried. "No! Don't! Put that down!"

"Don't be foolish!" Simon cried, sounding very alarmed.

"Eric, Craig, let's go back to our rooms. I'm really frightened," Cari whispered, trying to pull them away.

"Ssshhh—just a minute," Eric insisted, listening intently to the argument on the other side of the door.

"Edward—stop!" the woman screamed.

"No! I beg of you!" Simon cried, clearly frightened. "I beg of you! As a brother, I beg of you! Please—Edward—*don't!*"

"Guys—come *on!*" Cari pleaded.

She heard Simon scream.

Then, a second later, she heard the gunshot, deafening even through the heavy wooden door.

Then silence.

Chapter 16

A TERRIBLE "ACCIDENT"

Cari froze. Her breath caught in her throat.

She didn't realize how hard she was squeezing Eric's hand until he pulled his away in pain.

"Let's get out of here," Eric said, his face white in the dim hall light, his eyes wide with fear. But he made no move to leave. Craig's face had gone slack, his mouth hanging open, his breath coming in loud gasps.

It was still silent on the other side of Simon's door.

Dead silent.

A few seconds later the door to Simon's room burst open, and Edward staggered out. He gripped the hunting rifle in one hand, holding it out in front of him at arm's length. The rifle was smoking.

Edward's one good eye was wide with terror. He was wearing his usual outfit, the safari jacket, a disheveled sport shirt and wrinkled trousers. His white hair stood out on his head at odd angles.

Cari and the two boys took a step back, then another.

Edward seemed to be totally deranged. Out of control and dangerous.

He stormed out into the hall and slammed against the opposite wall. The four teenagers had stopped to huddle a few doorways down the hall. He stared at them as if not quite believing they were there, bewildered and wild with excitement at the same time.

"An accident!" he cried, his hoarse voice unnaturally high. "My brother Simon has had a *terrible* accident!"

He swung the rifle around.

Cari screamed.

For a second it appeared that he was going to fire at her!

But he continued swinging it in a wild arc, frenzied. "A terrible accident!" he repeated.

Cari heard rapid footsteps coming up the stairs. A few seconds later Martin appeared, wearing a dark robe and leather slippers, his hair tufted wildly about his head. "Edward—what is it?" he demanded. "What's going on?"

Edward, lurching unsteadily from side to side, bumping against the hallway walls, uttered a loud cry of despair. "A terrible accident," he told Martin. "Simon has had a terrible accident."

Martin's normally stony face seemed to crumble. His mouth dropped open. His gray eyes momentarily glazed over, then grew wide with fright. "Accident?"

"Call a doctor!" Cari screamed. "He's shot Simon! Call a doctor!" She started to open the bedroom door.

"Get out of there!" Martin shrieked.

Cari was so startled by his wild reaction, she stumbled into Eric.

"But Simon is hurt in there!" Eric protested to Martin. "And there's a woman in there too! We heard her!"

"Get away!" Martin cried, moving quickly to block the door.

"A terrible, terrible accident," Edward muttered, still staggering, seemingly out of control.

"Call a doctor!" Cari repeated. "How can you just stand there?"

"It's too late for a doctor," Edward snarled. He seemed more angry than contrite.

"What?" Martin cried, his face crimson in the dim hall light.

"It's too late. My brother is dead."

"How *could* you? How *could* you kill Simon?" Martin shrieked, his voice high and shrill.

"I *told* you it was an accident," Edward snapped.

Edward and Martin stared at each other, unblinking, challenging the other to back down.

Edward pulled the rifle in closer to his side.

Martin shook his head. He took a deep breath. "Edward, you know it wasn't an accident."

Edward didn't react.

"Admit it, Edward," Martin said angrily. "Admit it. It wasn't an accident. You shot him. Admit it. You shot Simon."

This can't be happening, Cari thought, staring at Edward, waiting for him to react. This can't be happening. Why isn't anyone going into the room? What about Simon? What about the woman?

"Admit it," Martin said more loudly, more firmly.

Edward stared back in silence, his eyes wild.

"That's quite enough from you," he said finally.

He raised the hunting rifle to his shoulder.

He aimed it at Martin.

"No! Oh no!" Cari screamed.

Chapter 17

A DISAPPEARANCE

"*P*ut down the gun," Martin said. His voice was calm, but he was trembling all over.

Edward didn't move. The hunting rifle was pointed at Martin's chest, less than three feet away.

"Put down the gun, Edward."

Cari pressed back against a doorway, huddled against Eric and Craig, too frightened to move. Would Edward shoot? His face was half in shadow now. It looked to her as if he were wearing a mask, one side dark and shadowy and terrifying, the other pale and uncertain and frightened.

"Put down the gun. You know you're not going to shoot me," Martin said. Even though he was trembling, he stood his ground, staring unblinking at Edward's shadowy face, and spoke in low tones.

Edward didn't reply.

To Cari, Edward's silence was more frightening than his rage. Was he going to listen to Martin? Was he going to lower the rifle? Or was he going to shoot?

Shoot Martin.

Shoot them all—

Kill them all, as he had Simon.

Edward took a step back, disappearing farther into shadows. He slowly lowered the rifle, but then raised it again.

"Let's go downstairs," Martin said coolly, not moving from his spot in front of the open door. "Let's go downstairs and discuss this, Edward. Let's talk this out, okay? We've always been able to talk before."

Will Edward do it? Will he listen? Cari wondered. She leaned back against Eric and clutched at his hand. She realized he was holding his breath too. She exhaled deeply and closed her eyes for a brief second.

"Come on, Edward," Martin said, his voice unsteady. Perspiration ran down his forehead. "You're keeping our guests up. It's very late."

"Very late," Edward repeated, his first words in what seemed to Cari an eternity.

"Let them go back to their rooms. You and I will go downstairs and have a chat." Martin glanced quickly at Cari and her friends, then returned immediately to Edward.

Again, Edward started to lower the rifle, then changed his mind. "None of your tricks!" he bellowed.

He's going to shoot now, Cari thought, squeezing Eric's clammy hand.

He's going to shoot us all now.

"No tricks," Martin said, holding out his hands as if to show there was nothing up his sleeves. "Just put down the rifle."

Silence.

Endless silence.

Then Edward lowered the barrel of the rifle to the floor and leaned on the stock. "It was just an accident. A terrible accident," he said gruffly, gazing back into the room.

"Let's go downstairs and discuss it," Martin said softly. Obviously relieved, he stepped forward and took Edward's arm. "You kids go to your rooms. Get away from that door. *Now!* I'll deal with this," he said and began to lead Edward down the stairs.

Cari sighed loudly and dropped to her knees.

"Ow," Eric groaned behind her. "My hand. You squeezed it into mush!"

"I'm sorry," Cari managed to say, her heart still pounding. "I didn't realize—" The hallway started to spin. She closed her eyes, willing away the dizziness.

"We've got to get out of here," Craig said, leaning against the wall. "He's crazy."

"What about Simon?" Cari asked. "Maybe he . . . maybe he's alive."

"And what happened to the woman?" Eric added. "Did she just disappear—like a ghost?"

"Oh no!" cried Cari, too frightened to think clearly. "Did Edward kill her too?"

"Come on—I don't care what Martin said. Let's check it out," Eric said, helping Cari to her feet.

She took a deep breath. And then another. It helped a little. At least the walls had stopped dancing in front of her eyes.

Eric led the way into the room, followed by Cari and Craig, who looked pale and shaken and was swallowing hard. "I've never seen a dead body," he said.

"Neither have I," Cari said, shuddering.

The room smelled of death.

Gunpowder and sweat. And death.

The three teenagers found themselves in a large sitting room, furnished in white leather and chrome, not at all the rustic style of the rest of the hotel. A long, sleek couch was flanked by an armchair and a recliner, all modern and white. A low glass coffee table in front of the couch held a silver teapot and several china cups, half-filled. A white wooden desk had been built into the wall behind the couch.

Two doors against the back wall appeared to lead to other rooms. "It's a suite," Eric said, his eyes ranging around the large room. "Maybe Simon, Edward, and the woman share it."

"But where *is* Simon?" Cari asked, forcing the room not to spin. She grabbed the back of the white leather couch. It felt cool and smooth in her hands and helped to restore her calm a little.

"They *must* have been in the front room," Eric said. "We heard them arguing here."

"Maybe Simon crawled into one of the back rooms," Cari suggested.

"But there's no blood," Craig said, pacing the

plush white carpet. "No sign of a struggle. No sign of *anything!*"

"Come on—let's check out the other rooms," Eric said as confused as Cari and Craig. Without waiting for them, he ran to the door on the left. Cari reluctantly followed, her throat tightening, dread making her heavy, as if she weighed a thousand pounds, as if she couldn't take another step.

She didn't want to see Simon's corpse. She didn't want to be there. She had a sudden impulse to run out of the room, down the hall, back to the safety of her room. But she didn't want to be alone either.

She took a deep breath and forced herself to step through the doorway. It led into a small, cluttered bedroom. A lamp on the bedside table cast yellow light over the room. An unmade bed, the covers wrinkled and bunched together at the foot, stood against one wall. Stacks of books and magazines and old newspapers stretched across another wall. Articles of clothing, all wrinkled and worn, were tossed all over the floor.

This must be Edward's room, she thought.

"Simon's not in here," Eric said, shaking his head. "Weird."

Cari tried to say something, but no words came out.

They hurried back to the sitting room and then tried the door to the right. It led to another, larger bedroom that Craig was already exploring. This room, Cari saw, was neat and pristine. The bed had been made and was covered with a beautiful antique quilt.

"Not in here," Craig said and shrugged. "No Simon. No woman," he said, dropping down onto the edge of the bed.

"But that's impossible!" Eric cried. "Cari and I heard them—"

He stopped in midsentence and turned to Cari, his face filled with confusion. "A body can't disappear into thin air—*can* it?"

Chapter 18

ANOTHER DISAPPEARANCE

"Have we entered the Twilight Zone?" Cari asked. She plopped down beside Craig on top of the antique quilt.

"Now wait a minute. Wait a minute," Eric said, talking loudly, rapidly, pacing back and forth in front of them. "We're just not thinking clearly. We've got to calm down. Got to think clearly."

"Eric—please," Cari pleaded. "You're making me even more nervous by pacing like that."

"Got to think clearly," he said, ignoring her, continuing to pace and think out loud. "We heard the argument from out in the hall. All three of them were arguing, remember? Then the gunshot. Then Edward came running out."

"Edward must have dragged the body someplace," Craig said, shifting his weight uncomfortably on the bed. "Eric is right. We're just not thinking clearly. The body is here. Somewhere."

"Let's do a better job of searching," Eric said, stopping his frantic pacing to see if the others approved his idea. "You know. Look under the beds. In the closets."

"No way. We've got to get out of here!" Craig said, his eyes on the door. "If Edward comes back and finds us snooping around here—well, he's still got the rifle, you know. And he's used it once already."

"We'll be fast," Eric said. "Come on. We'll split up. I'll take the messy bedroom. That must be Edward's."

"But, Eric—" Cari called.

Too late. Eric had darted out the door.

"Well, I'll search the front room," Cari said reluctantly. "But I don't think I'll find anything."

"Okay," Craig replied. "I'll look around in this room. The neat room. It's probably Simon's." He dropped to the floor and raised the quilt so he could see under the bed. "I just don't understand why—"

Eric's shout from the other bedroom interrupted Craig. "Hey—I found something!"

The words cut deep into Cari.

Had Eric found Simon's body?

The room was a blur as she hurried into Edward's room, Craig close behind.

"Look at this," Eric said excitedly as they entered. He was holding a large photo album in his hands. "This is really interesting. Look."

The others moved closer so they could see. "A bunch of old snapshots," Cari said, confused.

"They're all so dark. This album must be a hundred years old."

"Not quite. Look who's in here," Eric said. Balancing the heavy album on one upraised knee, he pointed to a photo glued in the upper-right corner of the page.

Cari and Craig squeezed closer to get a better view.

Cari recognized the front of the hotel in the old photograph. The Howling Wolf Inn hadn't changed a bit. A big sedan in front of the main entrance looked as if it were from the fifties. It was a spring day. A young man and woman stood leaning against the fancy car.

"Why, that's Simon," Cari said. "I hardly recognized him with black hair."

"Yeah, he looks exactly the same, except for the hair," Eric said. "And look who's with him."

"It's Jan's Aunt Rose!" Cari exclaimed. "Let me read what it says." She pulled the book away from Eric to read the caption that someone had written in bold black ink.

"My distant cousin Rose. I wish we weren't so distant."

"Distant cousin?" Cari's face filled with disbelief as she handed the heavy album back to Eric.

"Rose and Simon Fear are cousins," Eric said.

The three of them considered this for a few seconds. "That means that Rose and Edward are also cousins," Cari said thoughtfully. She glanced up from the photo album at the two boys. "You don't suppose . . ."

"That Rose knew what was going on here?" Eric

finished her thought for her. "That Rose knew what a frightening place this was?"

"Maybe she wasn't really sick!" Craig added excitedly. "Maybe Rose was working with Edward. And Martin too. Maybe Rose lured us here for some reason."

"And that's why Jan hasn't been able to reach her," Eric said. "That's why Rose hasn't called. She knew about this place. She must be working with Edward to—"

"Whoa!" Cari cried. "Cool your jets. Let's not get carried away. We have no reason to suspect Rose."

"But why didn't she ever mention that she's a Fear?" Craig asked. "Why didn't she ever tell us? Why did she keep it a secret?"

"Craig is right," Eric agreed quickly. "She deliberately didn't tell us that she's related—in some way—to the two Fear brothers."

"Hey—that means Jan is related to them too!" Cari suddenly realized.

"No wonder she's so interested in ghosts and creepy things," Craig said.

"Maybe Jan has been in on the plan too," Eric said thoughtfully. "Maybe she and her aunt *both* lured us here."

"But why?" Cari asked. "I can't imagine why—"

A noise from the hallway made Eric drop the photo album. It hit the floor with a loud thud that almost made Cari's heart stop.

"Ohh!"

They froze in place and listened.

No one came in.

"We've got to get out of here," Craig pleaded.

"Craig's right. We're not accomplishing anything by looking at an old photo album," Cari said to Eric. "We've got to call the police on Willow Island. Let *them* search the rooms."

"Maybe there's a trapdoor somewhere in here," Eric said, not listening to her. "Edward shot Simon. Then he pulled the trapdoor and Simon slid out of sight."

"But there's no blood," Craig said. "No blood at all."

"Come on," Cari pleaded. "Let's get out of here. Eric, are you coming?"

"In a second," he said. He was tapping the walls, turning the lamps around, pressing dresser-drawer knobs.

"What are you doing?" Cari asked.

"Trying to find how to open the trapdoor," Eric said. He flicked the light switch in front of him on the wall.

"Whoa! Look out!"

The bookshelves against the wall began to revolve as if on a turntable. As they turned, they revealed a desk on the other side.

Eric flicked the switch again. The turntable stopped halfway around. Everyone stared, frozen in surprise for a moment. "Look—there's a secret room back there!" Eric cried.

He squeezed into the space between the wall and the desk. "It's like a study. A hidden study back here."

"Is the body there?" Cari cried. She and Craig

136

peered into the hidden room, but it was too dark to see.

"No. No body," Eric said. He had picked up a sheet of paper from the desk. "Whoa. Hold on," he said, coming back into the room.

His face went pale. His eyes grew wide with disbelief.

"Eric, what is it?" Cari cried. "What's the matter?"

He handed the sheet of paper to her.

It was a letter, written by hand in blue ink. "It's a letter to Jan's aunt," she said. "Listen. I'll read it out loud."

She started to read the letter to Craig and Eric in a normal, steady voice. But as its contents became clear, her voice began to tremble.

"'Dear Rose,'" the letter began. "'I am so sorry to tell you that I fear a terrible tragedy has occurred. Your niece Jan and her three friends have disappeared without a trace, without an explanation.

"'I have been frantic, wracked with sadness, with fear, with remorse. The police from Willow Island have combed every inch of the island, without success. Without a single clue.

"'I've been trying to call you night and day. You didn't answer your phone. So I am sending this letter special delivery.

"'So sorry to send such tragic news by mail. I am saddened and mystified. I pray that the four young people will turn up unharmed. But the police offer little hope. I know that their parents will grieve, as I do. Rest assured that I am doing everything in my power to discover what has happened to them. I will not stop until the mystery of their disappearance is solved. I pray that they are alive, although all indications are that they tragically are not. I know that you will pray with me.'"

The letter was signed by Edward Fear.

Chapter 19

FOUR TROPHIES

"We've got to get out of here!" Cari cried, letting the letter drop to the floor. "He—he plans to kill us!"

"He's crazy! Totally crazy!" Eric said. He picked up the letter and quickly skimmed it again, not willing to believe what he and Cari had read.

"It's got to be some kind of a joke," Craig said.

"Get real," Eric told him. "It's no joke. He already killed Simon."

"Oh, my God! And Jan!" Cari cried, holding her hands up to her face.

"Shouldn't the police be here by now?" Craig asked, still staring at the blue handwriting on the letter. "Why hasn't Martin called the police?"

"Maybe Martin isn't going to call the police," Eric said thoughtfully. "Maybe he knows what Edward plans for us. Maybe the two of them are in this together."

"We can't stay here and discuss it," Cari told them, nodding toward the door. "Let's just get *out* of this place. Away from here—while we still can."

"Let's go to the dock and take Simon's boat back to Provincetown," Eric suggested. "You know—the boat he took to check up on Jan's aunt."

"I don't know how to drive a boat!" Cari cried.

"I do," Craig said quietly. "I've spent a lot of summers on the Cape. My dad and I love to go boating. If we can get onto Simon's boat, I'm sure I can pilot it."

"But what about Jan?" Cari cried. "We can't just leave her here."

"We have to," Eric urged, pulling her toward the door. "We don't know where she is. We'll get help. We'll get the police to come back and help us find her. But we've got to get away before Edward and Martin realize we know what they're up to."

A few seconds later Cari was back in her room. She tugged open the dresser drawer and began frantically pulling out her clothing and jamming it into her suitcase.

I've never been in danger like this before, she thought. Real danger.

What did Edward Fear have in mind for them? Did he plan to kill them? To keep them prisoner?

It didn't really matter. It was clear from his letter that he planned for them all to disappear—just as Jan had disappeared—and never be seen again. . . .

And what was Martin's role in this? she wondered as she jammed the last of her shorts and tops into the bag. Had he been trying to frighten them—or to *warn* them? And Rose. Could she have lured them there as Eric suggested?

Martin had told them again and again not to stay, to get out. Was it because he knew what Edward planned to do to them?

Too many questions, Cari thought, shaking her head as if trying to shake the questions all away.

She stuffed the last of her belongings into the bag, looked around the room for anything she might have missed, and, not finding anything, squatted down and started to fasten the suitcase.

I just want out of here, she told herself.

I just want out of here without one more scare.

And then someone grabbed her shoulder from behind.

Cari screamed.

"Oh. Sorry," Eric said.

She looked up at him, her heart pounding. He looked really embarrassed. "Sorry," he repeated. "I really didn't mean to scare you."

She clicked the suitcase shut and climbed to her feet.

He put a warm hand on her shoulder. "Are you ready?"

"Yeah," she said.

He kissed her. A short, tense kiss. "That's for luck," he whispered.

"I think we're going to need it," she said. "Where's Craig?"

Before he could answer, Craig rushed in, wearing the jacket he had arrived in, carrying a bag. "Let's go," he whispered.

Cari turned away from Eric and picked up her bag.

"Did Edward ever come back upstairs?" Craig asked.

"I don't know. I didn't hear anything," Cari said.

"Neither did I," said Eric, peering out into the hall.

"We'd better not risk going past his room," Craig said.

"But the stairway—" Cari started.

"Craig's right," Eric said. "We'll go another way. There's bound to be a back stairway that leads to the back of the hotel. Once we're outside, we'll just circle around to the front."

"I think we should call the police before we go," Craig said. "I-I'd feel a lot safer knowing that the police from Willow Island were on their way."

"No, let's just get *out* of here," Eric said impatiently.

"I think Craig's right," Cari said, nervously checking the door. "We could tell them about Jan. Also, what if we get caught sneaking away? What if Edward or Martin stop us? Then at least we could tell them we called the police. It might save our lives."

"But the nearest phone is in the front lobby," Eric protested.

"There's a phone in back. By the kitchen," Craig said, shifting his big canvas bag to his other hand. "I remember seeing it. If we go down the back way, we can call from there. It'll only take a second."

"Okay, okay," Eric reluctantly agreed. "But let's

just get going. By the time we finish discussing everything, Edward will be up here."

Without another word, they crept out into the dim light of the hallway. Cari took a deep breath. The air was hot and thick, making it hard to breathe.

Or was it just because she was so scared?

So scared that she had to concentrate just to get her legs to move.

So scared that every creak of the floor, every shifting shadow on the wall, sent a stab of terror up her spine.

They turned away from Edward's room, turned a corner into a long corridor that led toward the back of the hotel. Doors lined the right side of the corridor, most of them open, the rooms behind them dark and silent. Several of the small lamps on the left wall were out so that this corridor was even darker than the last.

"Are we going the right way?" Craig whispered.

"Sshhhh," Cari whispered nervously. She stopped suddenly and turned to look behind them.

She just had a feeling, a feeling they were being followed.

"Cari, what's wrong?" Eric whispered.

"Nothing. Sorry," she whispered back.

There was no one there. She shrugged and followed Eric.

They turned another corner, into another hot, musty-smelling corridor lined with rooms on only one side.

We're never getting out of here, Cari thought.

We're going to be walking in circles in this dark maze of hallways forever.

"Shh—look!" Eric whispered, pointing.

At the end of the corridor, a door was partially open, and light poured out from the room inside.

The three of them stopped. And listened.

Was the room occupied?

The only sounds were their own breathing.

They moved forward slowly, cautiously. "I don't think I've ever been down here," Cari whispered to Eric.

They stopped a few feet from the door and listened again.

Silence.

"Maybe there's a phone in there. We could call the police," Craig whispered.

Mustering her courage, Cari stepped up to the doorway and poked her head into the room. It took her eyes a second to adjust to the bright light.

"Wow," she mouthed silently.

"What is it?" Eric asked eagerly. He stepped up beside her and peered in also.

They stepped into the brightly lit room, nervously checking all around them.

"It's some sort of trophy room," Cari said.

"Yeah. Look at the hunting trophies," Eric said, picking up a silver cup. It had a hunter and a hound etched into its side.

"I don't see a phone," Craig said, sounding very disappointed.

"This is weird," Eric said. "Way weird." He stepped up to a glass display case, admiring the brass and silver trophies inside.

"Let's go," Craig said impatiently, starting toward the door. "Who cares about a bunch of hunting trophies? So *what* if people like to hunt at this hotel?"

"Yes, let's get—" Cari started, but abruptly stopped. Her mouth dropped open, and she gasped in horror.

"Look—" she cried.

She was staring past the glass display cases to the far wall.

Mounted high on the wall, much like deer or moose heads, were four heads.

Four human heads.

Chapter 20

BOAT PROBLEMS

*I*nto the warm night.

The symphony of crickets. The shock of the darkness.

The relief of being out of the hotel.

The fear that she wasn't far enough away yet.

Cari ran with the two boys through the tall grass along the back of the hotel. Everything seemed exaggerated. All of her senses were distorted. She could see every blade of grass, every clump of sand before her. She could hear the scratching crickets, the brush of the wind off the ocean, the hard breathing of her companions. She could smell the salt from the water, even smell the grassy dew that clung to her legs as she ran.

She could feel the fear.

The fear that had made them run from the hideous trophies, run blindly down the stairs and out the narrow back exit by the storage pantry, and keep on running without looking back.

Her bag felt heavy, but she didn't slow.

None of them did.

They turned the corner, breathing loudly, running at full speed, and headed past the hotel building, down the steeply sloping hill at its front, and onto the narrow private road that twisted through the woods down to the water.

"Ow! I've got a stone in my shoe!"

Craig stopped and dropped his bag onto the road and sat on it. Breathing heavily, he pulled off his sneaker and turned it over to empty it.

Cari, struggling to catch her breath, was grateful for the break. She turned to stare up the hill at the hotel, which was dark except for two lights on the second floor.

"I think we're going to make it," Eric said, wiping his forehead with the back of his hand. "They didn't see us. They're not coming after us."

Such a hot night, Cari thought. She was dripping wet.

Craig was gulping air. "We're not away yet," he managed to say, still trying to catch his breath. "We've got to get off this island. I won't feel safe till we're on the boat."

"You sure you can drive a boat?" Eric asked.

"Yeah. I'm sure."

"I can just picture you in a yachting cap," Eric said, grinning. "And the white pants and the admiral's jacket with those things on the shoulders. It's perfect."

"I can pilot it without a uniform," Craig said with a grim smile.

Cari still saw the four mounted heads in her mind. She couldn't stop thinking about them. They seemed to be following her, watching her as she ran through the night. "Those heads—" she said, to no one in particular.

"Try not to think about them," Eric interrupted, squeezing her shoulder tenderly. "Let's just *go.*"

"But were they—" She couldn't finish her question.

Were they four other people who had vanished on Piney Island? she wondered. Four hotel guests who never returned home? Had Edward written a letter to *their* relatives saying that they had mysteriously disappeared?

Cari tried to shut the hideous sight from her mind. She tried not to think about Jan. Poor Jan. But the four faces on the wall, their features stretched in horror, in agony, their hideous expressions trapped forever, followed her as she jogged with her friends down the road, through the whispering pines toward the water.

A few minutes later the tall wrought-iron fence came into view.

"We're almost to the dock!" Cari cried happily. Being so close to freedom helped her forget the aching of her arm, the heaviness of the bag, the fearful pounding of her heart.

Eric reached the gate first. He grabbed the gate latch and pulled.

He heaved a loud sigh.

Cari and Craig caught up with him. She could immediately see the despair on his face.

"The gate's padlocked," he said, breathing hard.

He tugged at the lock. He tried pushing it.

He slammed his bag against the gate. He put his hands around the bars and shook the gate as hard as he could, more out of frustration than as an attempt to get it open.

"We're locked in. We can't get to the dock."

"We can climb the fence," Cari suggested. But then she looked up at how tall it was and saw the spikes all along the top.

"No way," Craig muttered, dropping his bag to the asphalt. "The dock is so close. Just on the other side."

"Wait!" Cari interrupted. She had an idea. "We'll go back to the hotel—"

"What?" Eric cried. "Have you lost it? Edward and Martin must know we're gone by now. They're probably out looking for us."

"Wait—just listen to me," Cari said shrilly, unable to hide her impatience. She knew *her* idea was good. "I don't mean go *into* the hotel. We can run behind it and get down to the hotel beach. There are those canoes at the hotel dock. You know the ones. They're always tied up there. We can take them to get away."

"The canoes are on the bay—not the ocean. We can't take them around the island," Eric scoffed.

"No," Cari told him. "But we can take them to Willow Island. It's close, you can see it from the hotel beach. We can paddle to Willow Island and get the police."

"Now, that's a great idea," Eric said quickly.

"I guess so," Craig said. "I just hate the idea of going back up to the hotel."

"We'll keep to the trees," Cari said, picking up her bag and leading the way, leaning into the hill, forcing her legs to climb. "We'll stay as far from the hotel as we can. The lights weren't on in the back. It's pitch-black back there. They won't see us."

Her enthusiasm was catching. They picked up the pace as they made their way up the hill. The pale moon was just bright enough to light their way. Owls hooted softly from somewhere overhead. Again, Cari had the strange feeling that she could hear every sound, see everything around her with unnatural clarity.

The two upstairs lights had been turned off. The hotel was now completely dark. It loomed in front of them, a hulking black shape against a blue-black sky.

Walking through the tall grass that bordered the woods, Cari and the boys slipped past the hotel. The grass felt wet and scratchy against Cari's legs. She wished she had worn jeans instead of shorts.

The grass gave way to sand, and the dune that sloped down to the bay. She could hear the soft lapping of waves against the sand. Then she could see the bay, the moon reflected in its gentle waters.

They stopped just below the top of the dune, safely out of sight of the hotel. Cari turned toward the small dock where the canoes were always kept.

And gaped in disbelief.

And disappointment.

The canoes were gone.

She stared hard, thinking maybe they were hidden by the darkness.

But no. The canoes were not there.

"We're trapped," she said softly, reaching for Eric's hand, surprised to find it ice-cold. "We can't get off this island."

Chapter 21

EDWARD'S SURPRISE

The rain came without warning, a sudden burst that caught Cari and the boys by surprise. She looked up at the jet black sky. The moon was gone now, covered by low rain clouds.

A jagged streak of white lightning crackled out across the bay.

"I'm totally drenched!" Cari shouted over the rolling thunder that shook the dune beneath them.

"We've got to get out of the rain," Craig cried. "But where can we go? Do you think if we followed the beach we could walk all the way around the island to the ocean side?"

Another streak of lightning made the low rolling waves brighter even than in daytime. Cari brushed her soaked hair back with her hand, large raindrops running down her face, making it difficult to see.

"No, it's too far and the storm is too dangerous,"

Eric said, pulling at his wet T-shirt, his eyes on the sky. "The lightning's getting closer."

Another boom of thunder shook the dune. In the white light of the next bolt of lightning, Cari saw the tall grass sweep and bend eerily from side to side, as if trying to escape the storm.

"How about the pool house?" Cari suggested the accompanying thunder roared. The lightning was only a mile away now. The long, low pool house behind the swimming pool in back of the hotel housed all of the pool supplies and cleaning equipment. It would be a little cramped, but at least they'd be indoors, out of the downpour.

"Let's go," Eric said.

They started to run, no longer worried about keeping to the shadows. The ground was wet and soft. Cari slipped, stumbling over her suitcase, which seemed to weigh a thousand pounds now. She pulled herself up quickly and, dragging the bag in both hands, ran as fast as she could, following the boys to the low structure, praying that it wasn't locked.

It wasn't.

Eric pulled the door open, and they ducked inside. Cari was breathing so hard she thought her lungs might burst. The pool house smelled of chlorine. It was very hot, and the rain pounded deafeningly on the roof.

Eric clicked on the fluorescent lights and they flickered to life on the long, low ceiling. "No! Turn them off!" Cari cried, alarmed. "Edward—he'll see the light and—"

"It's okay," Eric said soothingly. "There are no windows in this place, remember?"

Cari sighed. Her hair was soaked and matted against her forehead. Even Craig, who always managed to look neat, appeared as if he'd been through a clothes washer.

"Now what?" he said, glancing around miserably. "Where do we go from here?"

"Is there a phone in here?" Cari asked. It was an outside chance, but worth a look.

They searched the cluttered building quickly, the three of them looking like strange water creatures, wet and green skinned under the fluorescent lights.

There was no phone.

"How do we get off this island?" Craig asked no one in particular, his desperation evident in his voice. "Edward has obviously locked the gate and hidden the canoes."

"Now why would I do that?" a gruff voice boomed from behind them.

Craig cried out in shock. Cari felt herself about to scream, but the sound caught in her throat.

She turned to see Edward Fear in the pool-house doorway, his hunting rifle in one hand, an umbrella in the other. He wore a long yellow rain slicker that came down to his ankles.

He tossed the umbrella to the floor and, leaning on the rifle, stepped briskly, purposefully, into the center of the room. His face looked livid under the fluorescent light, his white hair more unruly than usual, standing out about his head. He glared at them with his one good eye, his mouth twisted in a strangely pleased smile.

154

"Such a nasty night. What are you doing out here?"

No one replied.

How did he find us? Cari wondered. How did he know we were here?

"Well?" he demanded, the smile fading from his face.

A flash of lightning and an explosion of thunder made Cari gasp out loud. "We want to leave," she blurted out.

"Leave?" Her answer seemed to surprise Edward. Leaning on his rifle, he used his free hand to scratch his stubbly jaw.

"Yes. We want to leave the island," Eric said, finding his voice.

"But you *can't* leave," Edward said. He sounded almost hurt.

"We *have* to," Cari said. Edward had left the pool-house door open. The sky flashed behind him, immediately followed by the sharp crack of thunder. Sheets of rain now pounded the ground.

Edward was silent for a bit, staring at them, not moving from his spot in the center of the room. "You can't leave now," he said finally in a low voice filled with menace. "I'm formally inviting you to the party."

"Party?" Cari uttered, feeling the dread grow in the pit of her stomach.

"The party is about to start," Edward said, staring at her. He took a few steps closer to her. Cari tried to back up, but she was already against the concrete wall.

"Martin and I have been waiting for the party to

start," Edward said, his strange smile returning. "Guess what kind of party it is."

"Please—we just want to *go!*" Cari cried, feeling on the verge of tears. "We won't tell anyone about Simon or anything. We promise. We just want to go home."

"Guess what kind of party it is," Edward repeated, ignoring Cari's plea. He didn't wait for any guesses. "Give up? It's a *hunting* party!" He laughed, a loud cackle. "And guess who Martin and I are going to be hunting this season!" He laughed again.

Cari felt chilled through and through. "No!" she cried out, picturing the four heads, the four human heads, mounted on the trophy-room wall.

She understood what Edward meant. They all did. They all understood what kind of hunting party Edward had in mind. And they all understood immediately that they were the *prey*.

"This is *crazy!*" Cari cried. *"You're* crazy!"

She didn't even realize she was saying it. The words just exploded out of her.

Edward raised the hunting rifle in response.

Cari cried out and tried to edge away. But there was nowhere to hide.

"You shouldn't have said that," Edward said angrily. "I invited you to a party. You shouldn't insult me."

"Let us out of here!" Eric demanded.

"I'm *not* crazy," Edward said, ignoring him. He raised the rifle higher, aimed it at Cari, and took two steps closer to her.

"No—please—" Cari screamed. Without thinking about it, she plunged forward and batted at the barrel of the rifle.

The rifle went off, a fiery explosion.

Edward cried out, staggered, and toppled backward. His head hit the corner of a wooden picnic table as he fell.

Cari and her two friends didn't wait for Edward to get up.

Leaving their bags behind, they scrambled past him to the door and out into the driving rain.

PART THREE

THE
PARTY

Chapter 22

EDWARD TAKES AIM

"This way!" Eric yelled.

Her sneakers slipping on the wet sand, Cari followed him into the woods. "Hurry!" she said to Craig and tried to peer through the darkness to the pool house. Edward still hadn't emerged.

Into the safety of the woods.

The three of them, running, slowed their pace only a little to follow the twisted path through the trees. The rain had turned to a drizzle, but a fresh burst of large cold drops fell onto them every time a gust of wind shook the leaves.

Like rifle fire, Cari thought.

Rifle fire hailing down.

The clouds parted just then for the pale moon to show through the treetops, making the woods silvery and ghostlike. The leaves shimmered eerily, wisps of mist rose damp and warm around them.

"Where are we going?" Craig called.

"Just keep running," Cari said, breathing hard. "Ouch!"

A twig on a low tree branch snapped hard against her forehead. She stopped, stunned by the sudden stab of pain. Rubbing the spot, she realized she was okay.

A gust of wind sent down another volley of raindrops from the trees. She ducked away, too late, and was completely drenched.

They ran a bit farther into the woods. The path ended suddenly, and brambles rose up menacingly, blocking their way.

"Where are we going?" Craig repeated, sounding a little more frantic. "Stop! Come *on*—where are we going?"

They stopped and huddled together under a wide tree. The ground is dry here, Cari realized. The trees were so thick, the rain couldn't get down to them. She struggled to catch her breath.

A tremor of wind. The leaves seemed to shiver.

"Is he coming?" Craig asked, pressing both hands against the rough bark of the tree.

They all listened.

The only sounds were the eerie whispers of the wind and their own heavy breathing.

"He's going to hunt us down," Cari blurted out. "Like animals."

She pictured again the four heads on the wall of the trophy room. The four human heads, their expressions frozen in horror.

Were they the victims of Edward's *last* hunting party?

"We can't just keep running," she told them,

wiping the warm perspiration off her forehead with the sleeve of her T-shirt. "We need a plan."

"We've got to get off this island," Craig said, searching behind him, his face reflecting his fear.

"We've already tried that," Eric said, tugging nervously at his ponytail. He slapped at a mosquito on his arm. "We can't get off the island without a boat."

"We'll build a canoe out of tree bark," Cari said. "Isn't that what the Indians did?"

"Very helpful," Eric muttered. Despite his fear, he smiled at her. "You have a weird sense of humor."

"Just trying to keep it together," Cari said, realizing she could lose the struggle at any moment, fall apart, let the fear take over. At least the rain had stopped.

"We've got to call the police," Eric said. "Willow Island is only ten minutes away. If only . . ." His voice trailed off.

"All the phones are back at the hotel," Cari said, slapping a mosquito on her knee.

"So we'll go back there," Eric said.

"You're not serious," Craig exclaimed.

"Yes, I am. We'll sneak back to the hotel and call the police."

"But what if Edward or Martin—" Craig started.

"That's the last place they'll look for us—right?" Eric asked.

"I'm not so sure," Cari said, rubbing the fresh mosquito bite that swelled on her knee. "We don't know where Martin is, do we?"

"They're probably both coming after us," Craig said, his voice trembling. "Hunting us down."

"So we'll double back, sneak into the hotel, and call the police," Eric said. "Then we just have to hide out until the police get here."

"Hide where?" Craig asked doubtfully.

"I don't know. In the hotel maybe," Eric said impatiently.

"I think it's safer hiding in the woods," Craig said.

"Safe for how long?" Eric asked.

"Eric is right," Cari said. "We can't just hide forever. We've got to do something to save ourselves, to get us away from this dreadful place, and to save Jan. At least if we get into the hotel we have a chance of phoning someone, of getting help."

After a few more seconds of whispered discussion, they all agreed to the plan. "We should stay off the path on the way back," Cari said as they started walking quickly in the direction of the hotel.

A burst of wind brought another shower of water down on them.

And then they heard the rifle shot.

And saw Edward just ahead, between two low trees; his rifle was aimed at them, poised to explode in another shot.

Chapter 23

A GHOST APPEARS

The second rifle shot echoed off the trees.

It seemed to come at them from all directions at once.

She wanted to scream, but managed somehow to stifle it. She ducked, her knees hitting the ground hard, and crawled with her friends into the overgrowth.

Then, without exchanging a word, the three of them were on their feet again and running, running at full speed, slapping the branches away with both hands.

Another rifle shot.

From close behind them.

It was followed by loud, harsh laughter.

Or did Cari imagine that?

In her terror, suddenly nothing was real. Not the bushes that blocked her path. Not the slippery, marshy ground. Not the shimmering, silvery leaves on trees that circled her, that seemed to move with her. Not the rifle shot so near, so loud, nor its ricocheting echoes.

Not the mad laughter.

Edward's horrifying hunting cry . . .

"Hey—look where we are!" Cari cried, not recognizing her high, tight, breathless voice.

They had run through the woods to the ocean. Tall waves, outlined gold by the moonlight, crashed violently against the shadowy blue sand.

They stopped and stared at the water. The beach was flat and narrow here. There were no dunes to hide behind.

"We can't stay here," Cari said.

"You're right. It's too exposed," Eric quickly agreed.

They stood and caught their breath, listening for Edward, for another crack of the rifle.

"What now?" Craig asked, perspiration running down his forehead. Some wet leaves had become tangled in his hair. He hadn't bothered to pull them off.

"Let's keep to the plan and go back to the hotel," Cari said.

"Cari's right," Eric agreed. His T-shirt was soaked through. "We're sitting ducks out here."

"What was that sound?" Craig cried.

They froze, listening hard.

The waves crashed loudly against the shore, a continuous roar. Nothing else.

No rifle fire. No ricocheting echoes.

No mad laughter beyond the trees.

166

"Let's go," Eric said. There was no more discussion.

They made their way back into the woods, careful not to retrace their steps, careful not to follow any path, moving as silently as possible as they crept through the misty, hot night.

Like frightened animals, Cari thought.

Like wary, frightened animals, running from a hunter, running for our lives.

We're going to die, she thought suddenly.

We're going to be hunted down. And we're going to be murdered.

She hadn't even realized that she'd stopped moving, that the others had continued on ahead. Her legs suddenly felt so weak.

I'm going to die. We're all going to die.

Her legs just wouldn't cooperate. She felt shaky all over.

I can't move.

I can't move another inch.

Edward is going to find me here, like a frightened rabbit, paralyzed by fear. He's going to find me here and shoot me.

And then he's going to laugh.

She shifted her eyes and saw that she was alone. Where were the others?

They've left me here to die.

No. That couldn't be. That was impossible. They wouldn't—Eric wouldn't—

And then she saw Eric coming back for her, his eyes narrowed with concern. And then he had his arm around her. "Cari, are you okay? What's the matter?"

"Nothing. I—" She couldn't talk.

She didn't want to cry. She grabbed Eric's arm and squeezed it hard, squeezed it until she had fought back the tears, the urge to cry.

"Let's get to the hotel," she told Eric, letting go of his arm. "I'm okay now."

And her legs started cooperating again. She followed him through the high weeds to Craig and the three made their way quickly to the back of the hotel.

Moving silently along the wide stretch of beach, they looked up at the old hotel, hovering on the hill above them.

Has Edward returned to the hotel too? Cari wondered. Is he waiting up there for us, waiting with his rifle loaded? Is that why all the lights have been turned off?

And what about Martin? Has he joined the hunting party too?

Is Edward stalking us in the woods while Martin waits to trap us in the hotel?

"Spread out," Cari whispered. They were huddled so closely together, she realized, a couple of bullets could get them all!

Reluctantly, they moved away from one another and, crouching low, a relentless wind on their backs, climbed the hill that led to the back terrace.

The pool-house door had been left open, Cari saw. But the lights were off now.

All lights everyplace had been turned out.

Edward obviously liked to conduct his hunting parties in the dark.

A loud crash nearby made her cry out. Her chest

felt as if it might explode. Everything went white for a moment, and she struggled to breathe.

Just a deck chair, she realized. Just a deck chair blown over by the wind.

All three of them froze in place just beyond the swimming pool and listened. Would the sound of the falling chair draw the attention of Edward or Martin?

They waited. And listened.

Another deck chair, victim of the gusting winds, toppled over.

No movement from the hotel. No sign of their hunters.

"Let's go." Eric motioned for them to follow him. Cari took a deep breath and moved silently across the terrace to the dining-room door.

A few seconds later they were inside the dark dining room. For some reason the air felt cooler inside. Moving silently, they walked past the scaffolding, past their unfinished work, work they would never finish now, toward the double doors to the lobby.

"No one's around," Craig whispered, right behind Cari.

"They must both be out in the woods," Eric whispered.

"Let's hope," Cari said, realizing she had her fingers crossed.

Flattening themselves against the wall, they made their way into the lobby. "We can use the phone at the front desk," Craig whispered.

Eric had already lifted the receiver to his ear. He listened for a few seconds. "No dial tone," he whispered, handing the receiver to Cari, as if he needed a witness to the truth.

"No phone? I don't *believe* it!" Craig cried, forgetting to whisper.

Cari held the phone to her ear. It clicked a few times. Then she breathed a sigh of relief as she heard the steady hum of the dial tone. "It just clicked in," she told Eric.

"Quick—" Eric said, his hand on her shoulder. "Get the Willow Island police." His eyes darted nervously around the darkened lobby.

"Operator," a man's nasal voice said in Cari's ear.

"Willow Island police," Cari said, her voice wavering.

"Is this an emergency?" the nasal voice asked, sounding almost suspicious.

"Yes," Cari told him. "Please—hurry."

"One moment please."

There was a long silence, then rhythmic ringing.

Cari stared at the front entranceway as she waited. If the door opens and Edward walks in, I'll duck under the front desk, she thought. Would she be safe there?

Not for long . . .

"Police." The voice was surprisingly deep, startling Cari out of her frightening thoughts.

"Uh . . . hello. We need help. Right away."

"Calm down, miss. How can I help you?"

"You've got to send some men here. We're being hunted. We're trapped here and—"

Cari realized she wasn't making any sense. Her

fear was making it hard to think straight, to speak clearly.

"Where are you?" the deep voice asked with practiced calmness.

"The . . . uh . . . Howling Wolf Inn . . . on Piney Island. Please—you've got to come right away. We're really in danger. He's going to *kill* us!"

"The Howling Wolf?" He sounded as if he were writing it down. Slowly.

"Please hurry!" Cari repeated in a shrill, frightened voice.

"Try to stay calm. We'll be there in twenty minutes. Maybe less."

He clicked off. The phone went dead.

"They're coming," Cari told the boys.

"When? How long will it take?" Craig asked eagerly.

"Twenty minutes," Cari replied. "Maybe less."

"We just have to hide from Edward and Martin for twenty minutes," Eric said, sounding really relieved. "Then we'll be safe. Then we'll be out of this weird place."

"Where should we hide?" Craig asked.

Before anyone could answer, the lobby lights came on.

The office door at the end of the long front desk opened, and a smiling figure stepped out.

"No!" Cari shrieked. The others gasped.

It's got to be a ghost, Cari thought.

Standing at the far end of the desk was Simon Fear.

171

Chapter 24

TOGETHERNESS

Simon, in his white suit with a red bandanna draped casually around his neck, blinked against the sudden bright lights. He seemed to be confused.

He's as startled to see us as we are to see him! Cari thought.

No one said a thing for a few seconds.

"Simon! You're alive!" Cari cried, breaking the silence.

"What?" He gripped the side of the desk, appearing even more bewildered. "Alive?"

Cari and the others rushed toward him eagerly. "We're so glad to see you!" she exclaimed.

He was their only friend at the hotel. The only one who had been nice to them, who had welcomed them, who had not tried to frighten them or drive them away. And now here he was—alive.

Back from the dead.

Or was he?

"I . . . I didn't expect to see you here," Simon said, pulling nervously at his white mustache.

"Well, we didn't expect to see you either!" Cari cried.

The others laughed. Nervous laughter.

"Are you okay?" Craig asked, his voice filled with concern.

"I'm fine." The question surprised him. "Why wouldn't I be fine? What's going on here, anyway?"

"Well—" Craig started.

But Simon interrupted her with more questions. "What are you kids doing up this late? Why aren't you in your rooms? Look at you. You're all drenched! What on earth have you been doing?"

"You've got to help us," Cari blurted out, unable to hide her terror. "We've called the police, but—"

Simon eyed her warily. "The police?"

"It's Edward. Edward and Martin," Cari said.

"What? Where are they?" Simon asked. "What is that brother of mine up to?"

"Jan is missing," Eric broke in. "We can't find her anywhere. And Martin and Edward are hunting us. Edward chased us through the woods. He was shooting at us."

The confused expression softened on Simon's face. He rubbed his chin thoughtfully, staring hard at Cari. "Is it another hunting party?" he asked.

"Yes. That's what he called it," Cari said. "Can you help us?"

"You've got to help us!" Craig cried. "You've got to stop them."

"Stop them?" A strange smile crossed Simon's face. He took a step back, studying them. "Stop them?"

"Yes. They'll kill us. They really mean to kill us!" Cari cried. "But maybe you—"

She stopped when she saw the change that was coming over Simon.

Why was he grinning?

What did that strange grin mean? It distorted his face, made him look not like himself.

Why was he grinning at them like that, so . . . coldly?

"Simon, are you sure you're feeling okay?" Cari asked.

"Stop them?" The grin faded and he became menacing.

"Maybe you should sit down," Cari said to him, glancing at her friends, trying to see if they too noticed that something was wrong with Simon. "It-it's been such a strange night. . . ."

"Stop them?" Simon asked. "Why would I stop them?"

He reached up suddenly and tousled his white hair with both hands until it ruffled out at the sides. Then he tore off the red scarf and tossed it to the floor.

Cari and her friends watched in silent horror as Simon unbuttoned the top button of his shirt.

"Hey—what's the matter? What are you doing?" Craig cried.

"Please—" Cari started.

Ignoring them, Simon pulled off the white suit jacket and tossed it over the front desk.

They watched in horror and confusion as his posture changed. He was stooped now, leaning against the counter.

"Simon, please—tell us. What's the matter?" Cari urged.

What is that he's pulling from his pants pocket? she wondered.

It didn't take long to see that it was a black eye patch. He slipped it over his eye, his hands trembling with excitement as he fastened the band around his disheveled hair.

"Yes! Yes! A hunting party!" he cried in Edward's voice. "There's no way I can stop a hunting party!"

Cari gasped, frozen in horror. No one moved. They all stood staring at the grinning figure in front of them.

All three of them had watched the amazingly fast transformation. All three of them realized now that *Simon and Edward were the same person!*

Chapter 25

IT'S ONLY SPORTING

"Stop the hunting party?" It was now Edward who was facing them. All traces of the friendly, sophisticated Simon Fear had disappeared. Edward took a step toward them, threw back his head, and laughed. "You're asking *me* to stop the hunting party?"

"Simon—I mean, Edward—please!" Cari pleaded.

Edward turned and walked quickly over to a lounge chair across from the desk. He reached down to get his hunting rifle, which had been leaning against its side.

He's got us now, Cari thought.

It's over.

Edward raised the rifle in one hand. Then he held it in front of him as if studying it, wiping the dark wooden stock with his other hand.

Cari frantically searched the room for an escape route.

She and her friends had their backs to the front desk. The doors to the dining room were open, but they'd have to run past Edward to get to them. The main entrance to the hotel was across the lobby even farther away—and it was probably locked.

We're trapped, she thought.

We're dead.

The hunting party is over.

She thought of the four heads mounted on the wall. In a short while three more would join them.

She shook her head hard, trying to force the hideous picture from her mind.

Edward raised the rifle.

Where are the police? Cari thought. Can't they hurry? Shouldn't they be here by now?

Maybe we can stall him. Keep him talking until the police burst in and save us.

Edward checked the cylinder. "Loaded," he said to himself.

"You'll never get away with this!" Cari screamed.

It sounded so stupid. Like something from a bad movie. But the words just tumbled out. She was shaking all over now, her eyes darting from Edward and his hunting rifle to the front doors across the lobby.

"Can't we talk about this?" Craig asked in a voice so meek it barely carried across the desk.

Cari glanced at Eric and Craig, who were watching the front door too, no doubt hoping as she was that the police would come barging in. Craig, pale and terrified, had a glistening line of sweat above his top lip. Eric was grim faced and swallowing hard, his hands shoved into his pockets.

"Talk?" The idea seemed to amuse Edward.

"You're not just going to—going to shoot us . . ." Cari started.

He lowered the rifle. "Oh. Is *that* what you're worried about?"

He muttered something under his breath, then tore open his shirt a few more buttons. He scratched his chest with his free hand, leaning on the rifle with his other, glaring at them the whole while with his one good eye.

"Don't worry," he said, shaking his head. "I'm not going to shoot you now. Right here in the lobby. That wouldn't be sporting—would it?"

"Oh, thank God!" Cari cried.

Eric and Craig both whooped and laughed nervously.

Cari didn't relax. She knew there was no reason to trust Edward. He was crazy, after all. Totally crazy.

"So . . . you're going to let us go?" Eric asked eagerly.

Edward didn't seem to hear him.

"We can go?" Eric repeated.

Edward looked around the lobby. "Where'd Simon go?"

"Simon?" Cari asked.

Good, she thought. Maybe we can get him talking about Simon now. Maybe we can keep him talking until the police get here.

"Where is he?" he asked angrily. "That brother of mine, he never likes my parties. He's a bad sport, that's all."

"Simon doesn't like to hunt?" Cari asked.

Edward ignored her. "A bad sport," he repeated bitterly. "That's why I tried to get rid of him before the hunting party started. I don't want Simon spoiling the hunting party."

"Maybe we should look for him," Cari suggested, glancing at the others, hoping they were catching on to what she was trying to do.

"He'll turn up," Edward said with real bitterness, frightening bitterness, his expression truly ugly. "No matter how many times I try to get rid of Simon, he keeps turning up—like a bad penny."

"Are you going to let us go?" Eric repeated. He was standing right behind Cari now, one hand on her shoulder. His hand was ice-cold.

"Yes," Edward said.

"What? You *are*?" Craig cried.

"Yes," Edward said, smiling.

Cari suddenly felt very light, as if a weight had been lifted from her body. She felt as if she could float, float away from the hotel, from the island, float home—

"I'm going to give you an hour's head start," Edward said.

Cari crashed quickly back to earth.

"You're *what*?"

"I'm giving you an hour's head start," Edward said, studying his wristwatch. "When the hour is up, I'll come after you."

"But—" Cari started.

"It's only sporting," Edward said nonchalantly. "Martin and I are very sporting."

"Where *is* Martin?" Cari asked, her eyes on the front doors.

Police, where are you?

Where *are* you?

"You really don't have time to chat," Edward said coldly, checking his watch. And then, without warning, his face reddened with anger, and he screamed at the top of his lungs, "Get going! The hunt is on!"

"Edward . . . please—" Cari wailed, backing away.

Eric's cold hands gripped Cari's shoulders.

Edward, in a wild rage, raised the rifle to his shoulder, spun around, and fired once, twice at the lobby wall.

The explosions were deafening.

"No!" Cari screamed.

"The hunt is on!" Edward bellowed, white smoke pouring from both barrels of the rifle.

Cari and the two boys pushed away from the front desk and ran past the screaming, red-faced Edward, through the open doors into the dining room.

Chapter 26

ANOTHER GHOST

On the run again. Running for her life.

Cari lurched into the dining room, and darkness enveloped her. Trying to blink away the blackness, she felt as if she might suffocate, suffocate on the heavy, damp air, suffocate on the choking fear she couldn't run from.

All three of them stopped in the center of the room. Through the tall windows they could see the starless night sky, nearly as dark as the room.

Should they head back outside? Back to the woods?

That's where hunted animals belong, isn't it? Cari asked herself, bitterness mixing with her fear.

"Where to?" Eric whispered.

Cari looked back to the doorway to see if Edward was following. No sign of him.

Yet.

"How about the secret passageway?" Eric asked, holding onto Cari's arm.

"Yes!" Cari quickly agreed. "We can hide there until the police arrive."

The police. Where were they? It *had* to be more than twenty minutes since she had called.

"It might be safer in there," Craig agreed, sounding very frightened.

They moved quickly through the darkness, propelled by their fear. Cari got there first and stepped under the scaffolding to the door to the passageway.

"Hurry!" Craig urged. "If Edward or Martin sees us . . ."

He didn't finish his sentence.

A creaking sound from the far side of the room made them all freeze.

Was it Edward?

Staring into the darkness, Cari frantically searched the room. Her eyes were adjusting to the blackness. She could make out only the unmoving shapes of tables and chairs.

No one there.

"Just the floor creaking," she whispered.

Eric had the door open. The three of them slipped quickly into the passageway, carefully pulling the door closed behind them.

It was hot in the passageway, and extremely damp. It smelled of mildew, of decay.

Cari's back itched—both her shoulders ached. She had a sudden impulse to start running, to run blindly through the dark, twisting tunnels.

But, of course, there really was nowhere to run, she knew.

"We can hide, but we can't run," she said, not realizing she was speaking aloud.

Eric put a hand on her shoulder. "Are you okay?"

She couldn't help it. She laughed bitterly. "Okay? In what way? Define *okay?*"

She didn't mean to sound angry at Eric. It just came out that way. She apologized quickly. His eyes studied the dark corridor that stretched before them.

"Will we be able to hear the police from here?" Craig asked.

"I can't hear *anything,*" Cari said in a loud whisper.

"We need a flashlight," Craig said as they started slowly down the long, narrow tunnel, keeping close to the wall.

"Maybe you should run up to your room and get one," Cari cracked.

"Very funny," Craig muttered.

Pressed against the wall, they followed the tunnel. They moved in silence, listening as they walked, listening for footsteps, for Edward, for Martin. Every breath, every step, every sound was amplified to Cari, as if someone had turned up the volume control in her head.

She thought about Edward and Simon. How had he been able to fool them so completely? How could one person have both identities? The two brothers had looked so unalike, had acted so unalike, had even sounded so unalike!

If only Simon had won out, Cari thought. If only Simon had been able to drive Edward away. . . .

Cari scolded herself. These thoughts weren't getting her anywhere. Simon or Edward, or whoever he was, was crazy. Totally crazy.

And deadly.

He fired the hunting rifle in his own hotel lobby.

He didn't care. He didn't care what he wrecked. Or who he shot.

He only cared about the hunt.

He only cared about his prey.

Cari tried to force these thoughts from her mind as she continued to lead the way through the dark passageway.

And then she stopped.

Ohh . . . What's that?

Her face tingled. Something was tickling her face. Stringy things. Sticky stringy things.

They seemed to grab at her, choke her, enfold her as if trying to wrap her in a cocoon.

Cari raised her hands to fight them off, flailing the air wildly.

"Cari—what's wrong?" Eric called.

"Help me! Oh—help me!"

In her panic it took Cari awhile to realize that she had stepped into a massive tangle of thick spiderwebs. With both hands, she pulled at them, trying to clear them off her face. But they stuck to her skin, to her hands, to her hair. And the more she pulled, the more entangled she became.

"Spiders! Oh—help! I've walked right into those spiderwebs!"

"Cari, not so loud," Eric warned. "Edward might hear you."

"Spiders! Oh, please! The spiders!"

Eric helped to pull the cobwebs off her hair. She

shook her hands hard, trying to toss off the sticky webs, desperately rubbing her hands against her clothes.

And then she felt something on the back of her neck.

Something prickly.

Something moving, crawling down toward her shoulders.

She opened her mouth to scream, but managed to hold the scream in.

She slapped at it. Slapped it hard. Once. Twice.

She got it with the second slap. She could feel it in her palm. Warm and wet.

"Ohh." She shuddered. A spider. It had to be a spider. An enormous spider.

Eric and Craig huddled around her in the darkness. "Cari, are you okay?"

"Yeah. I guess," she said, feeling the darkness swirl about her, the endless walls close in on her. "I . . . I can't stand spiders!"

"Yuck," Craig whispered. "How big was it?"

"Big," Cari said, still shaking all over.

As big as a tarantula, she thought.

And then her mind flew off in another direction. We're caught in a web too, she thought. We're caught in Edward's sticky web. We're trapped here, trapped in his web, waiting for him to crawl over to us and finish us off. . . .

"Hey—this door opens!" she suddenly heard Eric call in a loud whisper, startling her out of her morbid thoughts.

Cari hadn't realized that the boys had moved a couple of feet down the passageway. She hurried up to them, her neck still itching, her whole body tingling.

I'll never feel normal again. Never.

They stepped through a doorway into an empty room. Eric tried the light switch near the door, and a dim yellow bulb, suspended from the ceiling, came on.

The room was small, but not so bare as the room that had contained the sticky skull. It had a double bed, Cari saw, and a nightstand, a two-drawer dresser, and a—telephone!

"Look—" she cried, scratching at her forehead, still trying to rub away the feeling of spiderwebs.

"Is it hooked up?" Craig asked, following her glance.

Cari reached it first and eagerly picked up the receiver.

Silence.

"It's dead," she told her friends glumly.

As dead as we are, she thought.

"Of course it's dead," Craig said. "The phones here all go through a switchboard, remember?"

"Huh?" Eric cried.

And they all realized at once how foolish they had been.

"You're right! The switchboard in the front office!" Eric said softly.

"All calls have to go through it," Cari said, still holding the dead receiver. "Including the call we made to the police on Willow Island." She replaced the receiver and dropped down onto the bed, weak and defeated.

"Simon came out of the office," Craig remembered, sounding as glum as Cari. "Remember? He had that odd smile on his face?"

"I get it," Cari said, shaking her head miserably. "I get it now. I wasn't talking to the police. I was talking to Simon the whole while."

"So there's no one coming to rescue us," Eric said, plopping down beside Cari.

"We're on our own," Craig muttered, glancing nervously toward the door.

"Aunt Rose," Cari muttered, staring up at the ceiling.

"What?" Eric asked.

"Aunt Rose. All the calls Jan made to her. Simon must have been on the switchboard then too. And I'll bet he didn't let those calls to Aunt Rose go through. That's why Rose and her sister never answered. He didn't want Rose here. He was happy she'd gotten sick. It meant she wouldn't interfere with the . . . with the hunting party, so he—"

"Let's move on," Eric said, standing in the doorway, scanning the passageway. "We're still too close to the dining room to suit me."

"What's the point?" Cari asked glumly.

"Maybe we can make it all the way to the beach," Eric replied. "We did it once before."

"What choice do we have?" Cari said.

Cari clicked off the light as she followed the others out of the room. The tunnel seemed even darker, even hotter. A sour aroma of decay hovered in the air.

"Look—" Eric whispered, pointing.

Cari saw it immediately—yellow light spilling

out from a crack under a closed door a few yards ahead.

They stopped, staring at the thin yellow line.

Cari heard noises from inside the room.

Footsteps. A cough.

"It's the ghost!" she declared, her eyes wide with fear.

Chapter 27

NOW THERE ARE
ONLY TWO

"It's the ghost," Cari insisted. She remembered the hoarse whisper following her down the hall, the eerie whisper calling her by name.

The three friends huddled close in the dark tunnel, staring at the thin band of light under the closed door.

"Ghosts don't cough," Craig said, unable to hide the fear from his voice.

"Maybe it's Martin," Eric suggested.

"It sounded like a woman's cough," Craig whispered.

"The woman in Simon's room!" Eric cried. "Come on—I'm opening that door."

"Hey—Eric—wait!" Cari called. "It's too dark. We've got to stick together."

But Eric ignored her and jogged toward the door.

Cari and Craig hurried to catch up to him.

Suddenly Cari heard a cry.

She and Craig stopped a few feet from the door. "Eric?"

Cari spun around. Eric wasn't at the door. Had they passed him somehow?

"Eric?" she called again.

"Hey—" Craig called in a loud, frightened whisper.

Cari gasped as she heard more footsteps on the other side of the door. Another cough.

"Eric—where are you?"

"I don't like this," Craig whispered right behind Cari. "Where did he go?"

"Eric? Eric?" Cari called.

She grabbed Craig's arm and held on tight. "Where's Eric? He's—disappeared!"

Chapter 28

THE VOICE BEHIND
THE DOOR

"He disappeared into thin air," Craig said, his voice filled with panic. "Come on. We've got to do something!"

"But where—" Cari started, but she was interrupted.

"Help me!"

"Eric?" Cari cried.

"Get me out of here!"

Yes, it was Eric's voice. It sounded as if it were coming from the floor.

"Where are you?" Cari cried.

"Be careful. There's a big hole in the floor," Eric called. "A trap of some kind."

Cari and Craig turned and found the hole in the floor against the wall.

"I think it's some kind of vent," Craig said, bending down. "Someone left the cover off."

"I don't care what it is," Eric grumbled. "Get me out of here!"

Cari and Craig bent down over the vent, grabbed Eric's hands, and pulled. A few seconds later he was standing beside them.

"For a little guy, you weigh a ton," Craig grumbled.

Eric started to reply, but was interrupted by a voice from inside the lighted room.

"Is somebody out there?" It was a woman's voice, muffled and distant, even though it came from just beyond the closed door.

"Yes! We're here!" Cari called.

"Help us! Please!" the voice called.

Stepping away from the open vent, Eric hurried over and tried the door. "Locked."

Craig moved up beside him and pushed against the door with both hands. The door seemed to give a little. "We can break it open," Craig said.

Eric pushed against the door, giving Craig a doubtful look.

"Use your shoulder," Craig said. "The wood is wet and weak. If we both hit it together, it should pop open."

Eric looked back at Cari. "Get ready to see your ghost," he said.

"Can I help?" Cari asked.

"There really isn't room," Craig replied. "Come on, Eric. Let's give it a try."

They backed up a few steps, then came lunging at the door, hitting it together hard with their shoulders. Both boys cried out on impact.

The door gave way easily.

All three of them cried out in surprise when they saw who was in the tiny room behind the door.

Chapter 29

NO ESCAPE FROM MARTIN

Jan ran toward them and threw her arms around Cari in a long, grateful hug.

"Jan! You're here!" Cari cried. "I don't believe it! I just don't believe it!"

And then Cari noticed the movement at the back of the small room. A very surprised and happy Aunt Rose stepped out of the shadows.

"Rose! You're here too!"

"How did you ever find us?" Jan cried, grinning through tears of happiness that ran down her cheeks.

"The question is, what are you doing here?" Eric asked, looking as surprised and confused as everyone else in the room.

"That's a very long story," Rose said, shaking her head. She gave her three rescuers a hug, one after the other.

"Rose, when did you get here?" Cari asked.

"The day after you did," Rose said, struggling to straighten her hair, which obviously hadn't been brushed in days. "I was feeling fine the next day, so I took the launch over. Simon met me at the dock and drove me to the hotel. But then . . . then he—"

"He forced her into the tunnel and locked her in this room," Jan broke in, seeing her aunt falter. "Only it wasn't Simon. It was Edward."

"He looked like Simon," Rose said uncertainly. "Of course, I hadn't seen Simon in at least twenty years. As I was telling Jan, he was quite handsome in those days. Simon and I are distant cousins."

"We know," Eric said impatiently, looking back to the doorway.

"That means I'm related to them too," Jan said.

"We know that too," Eric said. "Listen, a lot has happened. Simon and Edward—they're the same person."

"What?" Jan cried, putting her hands on her aunt's shoulders, as if for support.

"He's a split personality," Cari explained.

"Is that why he locked me in down here?" Rose asked, shaking her head.

"We don't really have time to explain," Eric said nervously.

"You've been down here the whole time?" Craig asked Rose. "You weren't the woman in Simon's room arguing about the party?"

"Woman? Party?" Now Rose was even more confused.

"Jan, how did *you* get locked in with Rose?" Cari asked.

194

"I . . . uh . . . Edward saw me. In the tunnel. I guess he was afraid I'd discover Rose, so he came to my room late at night. He grabbed me and took me to this room and locked me in with her."

"But what were you doing in the tunnel?" Cari demanded.

Jan's face reddened. She suddenly looked very embarrassed. "Uh . . . I think I owe you guys an apology," she said quietly.

They waited for her to explain.

"You see," Jan started slowly, "I knew about the tunnel before you three did. I'd discovered another entrance to it the night before."

"But why didn't you tell us about it?" Cari interrupted.

"I wanted to set something up to scare you guys," Jan admitted. "You know. Like the skull and the sticky protoplasm in that little room."

"Huh? *You* did that?" Eric cried.

Jan nodded her head. "Yeah. I found the skull in the tunnel and I thought I'd just play a joke. But then I got into it. I did all the ghost stuff here in the hotel. None of it was real. I made it all up. I put the skull in the little room. And that night we had the picnic dinner on the beach and I screamed and said I'd seen the ghost, I was making that all up. And I'm the one who followed you down the hall that night, Cari, whispering your name. And I put the sticky stuff on your doorknob."

Jan moved forward and gave Cari another hug. "I'm sorry. I'm really sorry. It was so stupid of me."

"But why?" Cari asked. "Why did you do all that? I don't understand, Jan."

Jan avoided Cari's stare. "I just wanted you to believe me. I was so tired of the three of you laughing at me all the time, teasing me. I just wanted to make you believe. You tried to act tough, but I *knew* I could convince you." A smile crossed her face. "I *did* have you believing it for a while. Admit it."

"Come on, guys," Eric said from the doorway. "We really have to get out of here. We made a lot of noise breaking down that door. If Edward or Martin heard us, they'll be here any second."

"Yes. We've got to keep going to the beach," Cari agreed.

"It's okay with me. I can't wait to get out of this smelly little room," Rose said. She took a few steps. Then her face turned white, her eyes rolled up, and she started to slump to the floor.

Jan caught her before she fell. "Aunt Rose?"

"I feel so faint," Rose said groggily, struggling to steady herself, leaning heavily against Jan.

Cari hurried over to help.

"She's probably weak from hunger," Jan said, looking very worried. "Edward only feeds us once a day."

"You'll never make it all the way through the tunnel. We've got to get you something to eat," Cari said.

"We can make our way back to the kitchen," Craig said, starting toward the door.

"But what if Martin or Edward—" Eric started.

196

"We'll have to take our chances," Jan said. "Come on. We'll grab some food for her and then go out the back way."

With the two girls helping Rose, they made their way back the way they had come, moving quickly but carefully through the dark tunnel. "Watch out for the spiderwebs. They're just around this corner," Cari warned.

They ducked low to avoid them and kept walking.

We're going to be lost in this darkness forever, Cari thought, supporting Rose.

But to her surprise, the door leading to the dining room appeared quickly.

Eric pushed it open a crack and listened. "No one there," he whispered. "Come on."

They pushed the door open just enough to slip out, and crept silently down the dining-room wall to the kitchen.

"Now what?" Craig whispered.

"It's too dark. We have to turn on some lights," Cari whispered.

It took Eric a while, but he managed to find the light switches. He clicked on one row of fluorescent ceiling lights.

The kitchen was clean and bare. The stainless-steel work counters had been cleared. Copper pans of varying sizes hung above the enormous range.

Cari had her eye on the kitchen door.

Were Simon and Martin out in the woods, trying to track the three teenagers down? If so, they would be safe here awhile.

But if Simon or Martin returned from the woods, they would see the kitchen light.

And then . . .

Cari and Jan helped Rose to a narrow rectangular table at the back of the kitchen, probably the table used by the kitchen staff for their meals. Making sure that Rose was seated comfortably, Cari hurried to the refrigerator.

"How about tuna fish salad?" Cari asked, pulling a large bowl off a shelf.

"Thank you, dear," Rose said, her face still colorless and drawn.

Cari carried the big bowl to the table, put it in front of Rose, and found a fork for her.

Rose ate hungrily.

Cari and her friends stood waiting, watching, listening for any sound from the dining room.

We've got to get out, get out, get out. The words repeated in Cari's mind.

Get out, get out, get out.

After a few minutes Rose put down her fork. Already she appeared to be stronger, some of the color had returned to her face. "Please, tell me what is going on here?" she asked.

Cari started to answer, but stopped.

Her mouth dropped open in horror.

Everyone turned to watch Martin stride into the room.

Chapter 30

OUT OF CONTROL AGAIN

"No! Get out!"

Cari screamed without realizing she had done so.

Martin stared menacingly at her, his black hair a wild halo around his head.

"Please—" Cari cried. "Let us go!"

Martin's face softened. Still staring at Cari, he suddenly appeared more confused than menacing. His gaze shifted and he saw Rose for the first time—his gray eyes wide with disbelief.

"Rose, is that you?! What are you doing here?" he cried.

"Martin, I could hardly believe it when I heard you were still with Simon," Rose said. "What's going on? Why was I locked up? Why are these kids so terrified?"

Martin sighed. His shoulders rose and fell. His whole body seemed to shrink and collapse. Cari noticed to her great relief that he wasn't carrying a hunting rifle.

"Simon is out of control," he said and shrugged, his narrow shoulders bobbing up, then slowly down, his hands lifting from his sides in unhappy resignation.

"Out of control? Martin, he greeted me at the dock, wild and unkempt. Then he led me back here to a smelly little room in a dark tunnel and locked me in!"

Martin shook his head. "I'm so sorry. I didn't know. You must believe me."

He quickly crossed the kitchen, took her hand, and squeezed it. He appeared to be genuinely distressed and concerned.

What's going on here? Cari wondered, watching the whole scene, still tensed, still ready to run, still wary of Martin.

There's no reason to trust him, she thought.

Why is Rose being so gullible?

"I can't believe he would keep you locked up," Martin said, sadly shaking his head. "Well, yes. I guess I can believe it." He let go of Rose's hand and slumped onto the edge of the bench.

Sitting hunched over like that in his black suit, he looks like a deflated tire, Cari thought.

Despite Martin's apologetic look, Cari found herself edging carefully toward the kitchen door. She glanced at Eric, who was standing in the center of the room between Jan and Craig, his hands shoved deep into his pockets, staring suspiciously at Martin.

"Well, you know Simon better than anyone, Martin," Rose was saying.

"More than thirty years," Martin said, his voice catching in his throat. "That's how long I've been employed by the Fear family. I've worked solely for Simon for the past fifteen. Sometimes I think of him more as a brother than as an employer." He sighed and then quickly added, "A very sick brother."

"Where is he now?" Rose asked warily.

"Out in the woods, I think," Martin answered quickly, glancing at Cari.

"In the woods?" Rose asked. "This time of night?" Without giving Martin a chance to answer, she launched into a barrage of questions. "Why isn't the hotel open? Simon assured me there would be jobs for the kids. Where are all the guests? Has he locked them up too?"

"I thought I could manage Simon," Martin said sadly, ignoring Rose's questions, his hands clasped tightly in front of him as he slumped on the edge of the bench across from her. "I was wrong."

He was silent for a long moment, lost in thought. Then he continued his story. "I brought him to this remote island because he had been so happy when we summered here. He was having problems. Serious problems. I thought he would get better. He was really enthusiastic about renovating the hotel. He sees a psychiatrist on the Cape, and I thought he was making progress. But in fact, he's gotten worse."

"Simon was fine when I knew him," Rose said. "I wouldn't have suggested coming if I thought—"

"I never knew he had asked you and the kids," Martin interrupted. "I did everything I could to get them to leave." He looked up at Jan, then continued. "I saw Jan snooping around in the tunnels. It gave me the idea to trap the kids in there for a while. I thought that would scare them enough to make them leave. I never dreamed you were in there too, Rose!"

Martin sighed and shook his head sadly. "It's all been since Greta's death," he said in a low voice. "Now Simon is obsessed, obsessed with hunting people. At first I thought it was just one of his sick jokes. He always had a twisted sense of humor. But his hunting obsession was no joke. And I foolishly played along with it. Even when he bought the wax heads to hang in his trophy room. I thought it was just a joke. Sick . . . so sick."

Cari heaved a sigh of relief. The human heads on the wall—they were only wax.

But her thoughts immediately turned grim.

We were to be his first real victims, she realized. His first *real* trophies.

"Why is Simon obsessed?" Rose asked.

"You know that Greta died in a hunting accident a few years ago," Martin said darkly, lowering his voice so that Cari had to strain to hear him. "He's been obsessed ever since. After Greta was killed, Simon's mind just snapped. Don't forget, they'd only been married a short time. It was too much for Simon, too great a loss. He couldn't deal with it alone. So he split himself into others. He began to assume other identities. To share the grief, I believe."

"He's a split personality?" Rose asked.

"If he was wild and unkempt when he met you at the dock," Martin told her, "he wasn't Simon. He was in his other personality—that of Edward."

"I see," Rose said quietly.

Cari couldn't help but feel nervous, standing in this open kitchen. She felt totally vulnerable. "Are you sure Simon is out in the woods?" she asked Martin, glancing out into the dark dining room.

"Reasonably sure," Martin replied.

"Shouldn't we go somewhere else?" Cari urged.

"There's no point in running," Martin said ominously, his face turning grim.

"Martin, what are you saying?" Rose asked.

"In his present state," Martin replied, "in the role of Edward, he's relentless."

"Have you called the police?" Cari asked.

"No, he's pulled the wires again. I tried to get to the Cape, to the police or his doctor, but Simon has hidden the dinghy," Martin said. "I've been out searching for it. That's where I've been the past few hours."

"And?" Cari asked, knowing the answer from the grim look on Martin's face.

"I couldn't find it."

"Find what? Is something missing?" a booming voice called out from the kitchen doorway.

Cari gasped aloud as Simon Fear burst into the room, hunting rifle in hand.

203

Chapter 31

MARTIN GOES FIRST

Simon was dressed as Edward, eye patch in place, the hunting rifle in his hand, his hair standing out from his head. His white trousers and safari jacket were wrinkled and mud stained, evidence of his long hunt through the woods.

After he stepped into the room and closed the kitchen doors, he slid a bolt into place, locking them all in. His eyes moved wildly from face to face, his expression mad and menacing.

"Simon—" Rose called out, jumping to her feet, one hand against the wall for support.

"Simon is gone," he bellowed. "Simon had no taste for the hunt."

"Go get Simon," Rose said firmly. "Go get Simon—now," she ordered. "I want to talk to him." Her voice was strong and certain, only her eyes revealed her fear.

Simon paused for a moment, glaring at her.

"Go get Simon—right now!" Rose commanded.

He stared at her a few seconds more, then turned to Martin. "What are *you* doing here?" he asked suspiciously.

"Simon—" Martin started, speaking very softly.

"I'm *Edward!*" Simon bellowed furiously.

"Go get Simon!" Rose repeated.

It was clear that Simon had decided to ignore her.

He shifted the hunting rifle to his other hand and began to raise it to his shoulder.

"No! Put it down!" Martin screamed, moving quickly from behind the counter and rushing across the room to stop Simon.

With a loud, angry cry, Simon lifted the rifle, flung his arm back, and sent the thick wooden stock crashing into the side of Martin's head.

Martin uttered a startled yelp. His eyes rolled up in his head. He slumped to the kitchen floor, his head snapping back and cracking on the hard tiles.

As Simon stared down at Martin's unmoving body, Cari and her friends lunged for the kitchen door.

"Pull the bolt! No—push it!" Jan screamed in total panic.

The bolt wouldn't budge.

Chapter 32

"SHOOT ME FIRST!"

It all happened in slow motion to Cari. She felt as if she were outside her own body, watching the scene in the kitchen from just above it.

She was just an observer, watching herself and her friends give up on the bolt that barred the door and turn back to face Simon. Watching Rose press against the wall, her hands to her cheeks, her face revealing her shock and horror.

Once Simon was certain that the four teenagers weren't about to escape, he looked down at Martin, who lay crumpled at his feet, his eyes wide open.

"That was some story you were telling them, Martin," he said, breathing heavily, noisily, the hunting rifle gripped tightly at his side. "Some interesting story."

He shifted his attention to Cari and her companions. "Too bad none of it was true," he said heatedly.

He raked his hand through his wildly disheveled hair. Then his attention flitted back once again to the unconscious servant. "You shouldn't tell lies, Martin. You shouldn't tell lies during a hunting party."

"Open the door, Edward," Rose called from her spot against the back wall. "Open the kitchen door and let everyone out."

"Why did you tell lies?" Simon asked Martin, ignoring Rose, giving no sign that he had even heard her.

He prodded Martin's side lightly with the toe of his boot. "Why did you tell such lies about me, Martin? I thought you were my friend."

He gave Martin a hard kick, then forgetting him, moved quickly to the four teenagers grouped around the kitchen door.

Cari quickly came down to earth, no longer an observer. She felt heavy now, heavy with dread, uncertain whether she could move from her spot.

"Martin has made it so easy for me," Simon said in Edward's gruff voice, a grim smile crossing his red face.

Cari stared at the hunting rifle.

"So very easy for me," he repeated, the smile broadening.

Cari stared at the rifle as it moved up to Simon's shoulder.

The rifle.

The rifle that he had fired at them in the woods. And in the hotel lobby.

"My own private shooting gallery," Simon said, very pleased.

The rifle was poised on his shoulder now.

Cari couldn't take her eyes off it.

"No—don't shoot them! Simon—Edward—don't shoot them!"

She heard Rose's terrified screams, but they seemed far away now, somewhere off in the distance.

Cari stared at the rifle until her eyes blurred.

"No—please—I beg of you! Don't shoot them!" Rose shrieked.

Simon aimed the rifle at Eric, then moved it to Craig, then back to Eric.

Staring at the barrel of the rifle, Cari stepped forward.

"Shoot me," Cari said in a voice surprisingly calm. "Edward, shoot me first."

Chapter 33

EDWARD SHOOTS CARI

Simon hesitated for a brief second, then trained the gun on Cari.

"It's too easy," he said with a dry, silent heave of a laugh. "It almost isn't sporting. But I gave you a chance. I gave you a head start."

"Shoot me first," Cari insisted. She took another step toward him.

He sighted through the rifle, then lowered it from his shoulder. His expression had become uncertain.

"Go ahead. Shoot me," Cari said, standing her ground.

Simon stood his ground too. But he lowered the rifle a little more.

"Cari, are you crazy?" Eric cried. He rushed forward and tried to pull her back.

She pulled out of Eric's grasp and stepped forward, her eyes on the rifle. "Give me the rifle, Simon," she said softly, reaching out for it.

"I'm not Simon. I'm Edward," he said flatly, without any emotion.

"Give me the rifle," Cari repeated, her hand still outstretched.

Simon stared back at her blankly.

"The rifle," she said softly but firmly.

His face furrowed in confusion. He lifted the rifle back onto his shoulder.

"The rifle," Cari insisted.

"Cari—stop! He's going to shoot!" Eric screamed.

"Okay, then," Cari said, staring straight ahead. "Go ahead. Shoot me. Shoot me first."

Simon aimed at her chest and fired twice.

Everyone screamed at once. But their screams weren't loud enough to drown out the deadly roar of rifle fire.

Chapter 34

RETURN OF THE GHOST

"Simon, give me the rifle," Cari said, sounding only a little shaken.

Simon's eyes popped wide in disbelief, and he nearly dropped the smoking rifle.

"Cari—" Eric screamed.

"The rifle, Simon. Hand it to me," Cari insisted.

His expression still stunned, Simon raised the rifle to his shoulder and fired it at Cari again.

Again, everyone screamed.

Cari didn't move her position.

"You—you're a ghost!" Simon screamed, backing away. "You're a ghost!"

He took another step back. White smoke from the rifle curled up to the ceiling. Behind him, Rose had slumped weakly onto the bench behind the table.

"The rifle," Cari insisted.

"No!" Simon cried. "If you're a ghost, then I'll have to shoot one of the others."

He took one more step back, raised the rifle to his shoulder, and pointed it at Craig.

"No, Edward! No more shooting!" a woman's voice cried.

At first, Cari thought it was Rose. But Rose was sitting half-dazed behind Simon, her head in her hands.

"I'll shoot if I want to!" Simon yelled in Edward's rough voice. "You keep out of this, Greta! This is my hunting party!"

"The hunting party is over, Edward," the woman insisted.

And Cari suddenly realized that the woman's voice was coming from Simon.

"Put down the rifle, Edward," Simon said in the woman's voice. "The party is over."

"No, Greta!" Simon yelled back in Edward's gruff voice. "Don't tell me what to do. I got rid of Simon, and I can get rid of you!"

"Edward, you're making me very impatient," the woman's voice replied.

It was the woman they had heard in Simon's room, Cari realized.

So there *was* no mystery woman in the hotel. The woman they had heard was another of Simon's personalities—Greta, Simon's dead wife.

When they'd heard that argument in Simon's room between Simon, Edward, and the mystery woman—*all three voices had been Simon's!*

"Get out of here! Get away from me!" Edward screamed.

"Not until you call the hunting party to an end," he replied in the woman's voice.

As he continued to argue with himself, three voices taking angry turns, Cari found herself staring once again at the rifle.

She took a deep breath and lunged forward, a desperate, off-balance leap. Magically, to her own surprise, the rifle came easily from Simon's hand. She grabbed it and kept running toward the back of the kitchen.

Simon was startled at first, but then he became angry. He lurched after her—

And tripped over Martin. He cursed angrily as he fell heavily on top of his servant.

Martin stirred and blinked his eyes.

Simon groaned and grabbed at his leg with both hands. "My knee. I hurt my knee."

Eric and Craig moved quickly to hold Simon's arms as Martin struggled uncertainly to his feet.

"What's happening?" Martin asked, rubbing the prominent dark swelling on the side of his head.

"Yes. What *is* happening?" Simon asked, suddenly switching to Simon's voice. "Why are you holding me? Where is Edward? I'll bet that brother of mine is responsible for all this confusion."

Simon sat up, but Craig and Eric kept hold of his shoulders. "Is the kitchen open?" Simon asked. "I'm famished. Are there any sandwiches available?"

The dinghy bobbed in the early-morning waters. The motor coughed, then dropped to a steady hum. Martin guided it toward the mainland.

213

Eric sat in the back, his arm around Cari. Jan and Craig were toward the front behind Martin and Rose. Simon, his hands tied behind him, sat by himself on the other side, staring down at the floor of the launch.

Cari took a deep breath of the fresh, salty air, then turned to take a last wistful look at Piney Island.

"How did you do it?" Eric asked, bringing his face close to hers so she could hear him over the loud hum of the motor and the rush of waves against the hull.

"Do what?" she teased, snuggling against him.

"You know. The rifle thing."

"Well, it was weird how it just struck me," Cari explained. "I was staring at the rifle and thinking about it. And I realized that he'd been really close to us in the woods, and he'd fired a lot of shots. But he hadn't hit us. He hadn't hit anything."

"Yeah? So?"

"Well, I decided he'd have to be a better shot than that."

"I guess. But that doesn't explain—"

"Let me finish," Cari said, gently slapping his shoulder. "Then I remembered about the hotel lobby. He fired the rifle twice in the lobby, remember? But there was no damage. Nothing crashed to the floor. No bullet holes in the walls. There weren't any ricochets. Nothing. That's when I realized that Simon's rifle was loaded with blanks."

"Weird," Eric said, shaking his head. "Really weird." Cari knew he was using it as a term of admiration.

"Martin was foolish enough to allow Simon his hunting party, but he took the precaution of supplying him with only blanks. At least, that's what I hoped."

Eric paled. "You weren't sure?"

"Pretty sure," Cari said. She reached her face up and kissed him quickly on the cheek.

"Party summer!" Craig yelled back to them from the front of the launch. "Party summer!"

Everyone laughed.

"Maybe it wasn't exactly a party summer," Cari said. "But just think about our great papers when it's time to write 'What I Did on My Summer Vacation'!"

Eric grinned at her. "You're weird," he said.

"Thanks for the compliment," she replied. "You're weird too." And she reached her face up for another kiss.

About the Author

"Where do you get your ideas?"

That's the question that R. L. Stine is asked most often. "I don't know where my ideas come from," he says. "But I do know that I have a lot more scary stories in my mind that I can't wait to write."

So far, he has written nearly three dozen mysteries and thrillers for young people, all of them bestsellers.

Bob grew up in Columbus, Ohio. Today he lives in an apartment near Central Park in New York City with his wife, Jane, and fourteen-year-old son, Matt.

THE NIGHTMARES
NEVER END . . .
WHEN YOU VISIT

NEXT: *LIGHTS OUT*

Something is very wrong at Camp Nightwing, and junior counselor Holly Flynn is determined to solve the mystery before it destroys the camp!

The trouble begins with frightening acts of vandalism. After each, a red feather is left behind—signature of the culprit.

Suddenly one of the counselors dies a grisly death. "An accident," say the police. But Holly knows better—and she knows she's next. Holly can't trust anyone now, not even her best friend, as she stalks the camp killer—and hopes that it soon won't be "Lights Out" for her!

R.L. Stine

☐ *THE NEW GIRL*............74649-9/$3.99
☐ *THE SURPRISE PARTY*.....73561-6/$3.99
☐ *THE OVERNIGHT*.............74650-2/$3.99
☐ *MISSING*........................69410-3/$3.99
☐ *THE WRONG NUMBER*...69411-1/$3.99
☐ *THE SLEEPWALKER*........74652-9/$3.99
☐ *HAUNTED*........................74651-0/$3.99
☐ *HALLOWEEN PARTY*........70243-2/$3.99
☐ *THE STEPSISTER*.............70244-0/$3.99
☐ *SKI WEEKEND*................72480-0/$3.99
☐ *THE FIRE GAME*...............72481-9/$3.99
☐ *THE THRILL CLUB*............78581-8/$3.99

☐ *LIGHTS OUT*....................72482-7/$3.99
☐ *THE SECRET BEDROOM*.....72483-5/$3.99
☐ *THE KNIFE*.......................72484-3/$3.99
☐ *THE PROM QUEEN*...........72485-1/$3.99
☐ *FIRST DATE*.....................73865-8/$3.99
☐ *THE BEST FRIEND*............73866-6/$3.99
☐ *THE CHEATER*..................73867-4/$3.99
☐ *SUNBURN*........................73868-2/$3.99
☐ *THE NEW BOY*..................73869-0/$3.99
☐ *THE DARE*........................73870-4/$3.99
☐ *BAD DREAMS*..................78569-9/$3.99
☐ *DOUBLE DATE*..................78570-2/$3.99
☐ *ONE EVIL SUMMER*..........78596-6/$3.99

FEAR STREET SAGA

☐ *#1: THE BETRAYAL*.......86831-4/$3.99
☐ *#2: THE SECRET*..........86832-2/$3.99
☐ *#3: THE BURNING*........86833-0/$3.99

SUPER CHILLER

☐ *PARTY SUMMER*......72920-9/$3.99
☐ *BROKEN HEARTS*.....78609-1/$3.99
☐ *THE DEAD LIFEGUARD*
............86834-9/$3.99

CHEERLEADERS

☐ *THE FIRST EVIL*.........75117-4/$3.99
☐ *THE SECOND EVIL*.....75118-2/$3.99
☐ *THE THIRD EVIL*........75119-0/$3.99

99 FEAR STREET: THE HOUSE OF EVIL

☐ *THE FIRST HORROR*..............88562-6/$3.99
☐ *THE SECOND HORROR*........88563-4 /$3.99
☐ *THE THIRD HORROR*.............88564-2/$3.99

Simon & Schuster Mail Order
200 Old Tappan Rd., Old Tappan, N.J. 07675

Please send me the books I have checked above. I am enclosing $_____ (please add $0.75 to cover the postage and handling for each order. Please add appropriate sales tax). Send check or money order-no cash or C.O.D.'s please. Allow up to six weeks for delivery. For purchase over $10.00 you may use VISA: card number, expiration date and customer signature must be included.

Name _____
Address _____
City _____ State/Zip _____
VISA Card # _____ Exp.Date _____
Signature _____

739-16